THE SIEGE OF TROY

ALSO BY THEODOR KALLIFATIDES

Another Life: On Memory, Language,
Love, and the Passage of Time

THE

Siege

OF

Troy

Theodor Kallifatides

Translated from the Swedish by Marlaine Delargy

OTHER PRESS / NEW YORK

Copyright © 2018 Theodor Kallifatides
Originally published in Swedish as *Slaget om Troja* in 2018
by Albert Bonniers Förlag, Stockholm
Translation copyright © 2019 Other Press

The cost of this translation was supported by a grant from
the Swedish Arts Council.

Production editor: Yvonne E. Cárdenas
Text designer: Jennifer Daddio / Bookmark Design & Media Inc.
This book was set in Centaur, Gill Sans, and Opti Lord Swash by
Alpha Design & Composition of Pittsfield, NH

1 3 5 7 9 10 8 6 4 2

Library of Congress Cataloging-in-Publication Data

Names: Kallifatides, Theodor, 1938– author. | Delargy, Marlaine, translator.
Title: The siege of Troy / Theodor Kallifatides ; translated from the Swedish
by Marlaine Delargy.
Other titles: Slaget om Troja. English
Description: New York : Other Press, 2019.
Identifiers: LCCN 2018059179 (print) | LCCN 2019000756 (ebook) |
ISBN 9781590519721 (ebook) | ISBN 9781590519714 (hardcover)
Subjects: LCSH: Troy (Extinct city)—Fiction.
Classification: LCC PT9876.21.A45 (ebook) | LCC PT9876.21.A45 S58513 2019 (print)
| DDC 839.73/74—dc23
LC record available at https://lccn.loc.gov/2018059179

Publisher's Note
This is a work of fiction. Names, characters, places, and incidents either are the product
of the author's imagination or are used fictitiously, and any resemblance to actual
persons, living or dead, events, or locales is entirely coincidental.

One

I WAS FIFTEEN YEARS OLD and in love with my teacher. The year was 1945, and it was the beginning of April. My village had been occupied—as had the whole of Greece—by the German army since 1941. The school didn't function at all during those years. The two teachers had been taken away by the Germans, and no replacements arrived. One of those teachers was my father. We didn't know if he was alive, or already dead. Mom cried at night and took care of me and our home during the day. It was just the two of us. Mom and me.

A retired lawyer sometimes gave lessons in history and Greek. Not in the school; the Germans had turned it into a barracks. We would occasionally gather at his house, but more often at his café in the square in the afternoons, as the lawyer tried to revive himself with several cups of coffee after his siesta. He drank them "heavy, without bubbles," which means without sugar and well stirred. It's not easy to say what we learned during those lessons, although we did become particularly adept at card games.

Miss arrived on one such afternoon, on the bus from Athens. The mayor came to meet her. She was a young woman, as thin as a strip of light, even though she was dressed in black from top to toe. I fell in love immediately, however weird that sounds. This was our new teacher, which was a good sign. Life would get back to normal again. But not for everyone. For me it meant that Dad would probably never return, and I prepared myself for even more sleepless nights with Mom sobbing in the room next door.

My only consolation was Miss. I never tired of gazing at her. She was small, dark, with burning eyes and beautiful hands, which she liked to move often. Officially we called her Miss, unofficially the Witch, because she could get the village's bad-tempered, cowering dogs to stop barking. Otherwise they would even bark at their own shadow.

It was Dimitra, my childhood playmate, who delivered the diagnosis.

"She's a witch," she said, and that was that.

The year was 1945, as I said. The Second World War was nearing its end, the German army was retreating on all fronts, but we knew nothing about that, and life in the village continued as normal. The German soldiers were no longer so alien, and there were fewer and fewer of them with each passing day. Some were killed fighting the partisans, while others were sent off to the Eastern Front.

With the permission of the German captain, lessons were now held in the school a short distance outside the village. That was where it all began.

It was a sunny day, the windows were open, we could see the German flag fluttering gently in the playful breeze. Miss was in the middle of explaining that transitive verbs require the genitive case, and gave a popular saying as an example: "Early each morning the happy housewife busies herself with her home. 'Her home' must therefore be in the genitive case."

"Bad example," muttered Dimitra, who had never seen her mom looking happy in the morning. She also detested all rules, particularly grammatical ones.

"Handcuffs for the imagination," she called them.

Miss took the opposite view. Her primary duty and pleasure was to teach us our language.

"Being Greek means knowing the Greek language," she said.

When we heard the roar of planes, we weren't worried. We assumed they were German. There was a temporary airfield in the village, built by the Germans for their transport needs during the Battle of Crete. Both my grandfather and my uncle had been forced to work there, like most local men. My father would have had to do the same, but he was stuck in some prison, if he was still alive.

We were sitting in the classroom when the first bomb fell, making the windows rattle. We were more curious than afraid, and rushed outside to see where it had landed. The first victim was a donkey laden with wood. Her big belly had been split in two, and she lay there kicking all four legs in the air as she slowly died.

The planes were not German. They were British.

The next bomb hit the school's primitive outside toilet, sending turds flying all around us along with dead mice and rats. Miss, who had come out with us, shouted that we must run to the cave if we didn't want to die.

We didn't want to die. The cave lay around a hundred yards from the school, a little way into a ravine that cut through the village. We all knew where it was. We used to play cops and robbers there, among other things, and we would sometimes spy on the courting couples who sought sanctuary inside.

The class consisted of six boys and just one girl—Dimitra. Seven of us. "A good number," Miss said. "God created the world in seven days."

So there were the seven of us plus Miss in the cave. It was cramped, dark, damp, and crawling with all kinds of bugs. We huddled close together. I sat right next to Dimitra. Miss went and stood in front of us in the opening to the cave; the light from outside fell on her, and she looked like one of the stern angels in the village church.

The bombs continued to fall. We heard explosions, the roar of the planes, the German siren, and then the bell ringer decided to take the opportunity to sound the alarm. He had loved sounding the alarm even before the war, when spontaneous fires would break out in the valley in the summer. His life acquired a meaning, so to speak, even if he went deaf as a result.

Miss seemed calm, and waited until our agitated chatter had died down.

"Listen, this might take a while. And that's fine by me. Ever since I was at university I've dreamed of this: having a class all to myself. There's nothing to do here, nothing to see. There's just you and me."

Dimitra was right; she was a witch. Our eyes grew accustomed to the darkness, we could see one another, and above all we could see Miss, standing before us in her black short-sleeved dress, her lovely white arms moving like gulls.

"When I was your age, an old man came to our school one day and read aloud to us from *The Iliad*, which you might have heard of. It's about the war between Troy, a city on the other side of the Aegean Sea, and the Greeks, or the Achaeans as they were called in those days. The man who came to us was a professional performer of epic poetry, a rhapsodist. He went around schools talking about Homer, who wrote *The Odyssey* and *The Iliad*, and reading extracts aloud. It is said that blind Homer did the same. He would travel from town to town declaiming from his poems, and people would rush out of their houses to listen to him. So I thought I would do that too. I will tell you the story of *The Iliad* from memory for as long as we're sitting here. It's not as if we have anything else to do."

That was true. We didn't have anything else to do in the cave, apart from trying to protect ourselves from the assorted bugs.

"So when was this war?" Dimitra asked.

"It was a very long time ago—more than three thousand years," Miss replied.

Dimitra sighed. "Can't wait."

Miss took no notice. I didn't think it sounded very exciting either, but as I said, we didn't have much else to do, so Miss began her story.

The sun was shining on the camps of the Achaeans, but their mood was far from sunny. In front of them loomed the high, imposing, and beautiful walls of Troy. They had been attacking those walls for almost ten years; many good men on both sides had perished in fierce conflicts. But the decisive battle remained.

The Trojans were fighting for their lives, the Achaeans for their honor. Perhaps that didn't weigh quite so heavily. The armies were exhausted, the men were missing their families, their homes, and their fields. Homesickness might not be a real illness, but it has the same debilitating effect on all of us. The men lost weight, their eyes and cheeks became increasingly sunken. Their teeth fell out, their mouths disappeared beneath mustaches, their breath could bring a dead serpent back to life, they suffered from chronic constipation or the reverse, their hair grew thin.

Their conversations were increasingly monotonous and vulgar. If someone scratched his head, someone else always commented that it was a sign of the cuckold's horns poking through. The wives were all alone back home, and everyone knew what could happen in those circumstances.

The men tried to keep up their spirits, but the songs they sang in the evenings were often mournful. The only thing that had improved over the years was the bond of friendship. They endured everything together, one man's shield protecting his comrade. One man's death frequently led to the demise of the other. As I said, almost ten years had passed, and the beautiful walls of Troy had proved impenetrable.

Things were different for the Trojans. They returned to their families after each battle, to their wives and children; their wives were famed for their slender waists, and with good reason. Proud and straight-backed in their long

7

robes, they were waiting by the door when their men came home. The marble bath was filled with water from mountain springs, warmed and soothing. The women washed the dust, the sweat, the stench of blood from their men, who were kissed and caressed and loved. That was how they had survived the siege for almost ten years, and they knew they could survive ten more.

It is one thing to fight on home ground, a different matter entirely to wage war in a foreign land. The question was not how long Troy could withstand the Achaeans' siege but how long the Achaeans could continue.

In other words, their leader, Agamemnon, knew that something must be done—but he didn't know what. A suspicion he dared not put into words, not even to himself, weighed heavily upon him. He summoned the other kings and generals to his tent.

They too had their suspicions. Almost all of them had committed one or more shameful deeds during those nine years: They had killed in stealth, robbed poor farmers, stolen away women and children.

Deep down in their souls, doubt was eating away at them. Was this a just war? Should they drown the city in blood simply because Paris, the son of King Priam of Troy, had seduced or abducted Helen?

Admittedly she was the most beautiful woman who had ever lived; she was even thought to be lovelier than Aphrodite herself, the goddess of love. One hundred and nineteen suitors from all over the world had courted her. Helen's father, Tyndareus, had not dared to choose one, for fear of war breaking out among the rest. Therefore he left the choice to Helen, while at the same time demanding that every suitor swear a solemn oath, promising that whoever Helen married, all the rest would defend that individual, and if anyone stole her away from her home and her husband, they would embark upon a war and lay waste the abductor's city, no matter whether he was an Achaean or a barbarian.

And so the great day came when Helen chose broad-shouldered Menelaus, King of Sparta. She went up to him and placed a wreath of early-spring flowers upon his fair hair.

It was a good marriage in every respect.

Helen and Menelaus lived a happy life. They had seven children, and she grew more beautiful with each passing day. It was said that the yellow sunflower and the blue chicory in her garden bowed down before her when she walked by late in the afternoon. The birds stopped singing, and even the great river Eurotas ceased its swirling so that she could admire her reflection in its crystal-clear waters.

It is also said that the devil has many legs, but the Fates have more. One day Menelaus received a visit from Paris, the son of King Priam of Troy. The two kings knew each other, so it was only natural that Menelaus should welcome Paris, who said that his ship had been badly damaged by a storm off the infamous Cape Maleas, and that he had been forced to abandon it.

None of them could have imagined what the consequences of this visit would be.

———————————

Miss paused and inhaled deeply, as if she'd been holding her breath while she was telling her story. She went over to the opening of the cave and looked out.

"Things seem to have calmed down; you can go home now. We'll continue tomorrow."

Dimitra and I walked home together. We'd known each other forever. We'd played "doctors and nurses," inspected each other's private parts. She was my oldest friend, and I was hers. We were like brother and sister.

"So what do you think of the Witch?" she asked.

I wasn't sure what to say. "She's got a nice voice."

Everything was back to normal in the square. The German captain and the mayor were enjoying a glass of ouzo before dinner. So were all the other men. Young women were strolling along arm in arm, allowing themselves to be admired. It was as if nothing had happened.

Two

THE NEXT DAY we went to school as usual, and Miss didn't waste any time.

"Shall we have a look at the verbs taking the genitive case, or shall we go back to Helen and Paris?" It was an easy choice, and so she began.

———————————

Paris wasn't just anyone. He was the son of a king, he was good-looking, and he had a heavy burden to bear. The night before his mother, Hecuba, gave birth to him, she dreamed of a flaming torch emerging from within her body. The seer who was immediately consulted informed her that this strange dream was a bad omen. The day the child was born was also regarded as ill-fated.

The only possible course of action was to kill the infant.

Priam didn't have the heart to carry out the deed. He had immediately fallen in love with the little boy with the blond curls. He handed him over to his herdsman, who couldn't bring himself to kill the child either, but left him in the forest to die. Nine days later he went back to make sure the baby was dead, and found him being suckled by a she-bear.

The herdsman lifted his gaze to the sky. The gods wanted this child to live. He took him home, intending to raise him as his own, and returned to Priam with the tongue of a dog as proof that the king's orders had been carried out.

The years passed. Paris grew into an unusually handsome young man, and the rumor spread that he wasn't in fact the son of the herdsman, who looked more like the goats he tended. One day a young princess came along. Her name was Cassandra, and she was Priam's pride and joy. The god Apollo had bestowed on her the gift and the curse of seeing what no one else could see, and she knew immediately that the handsome young man was her brother. Together they went to her father's palace, where the celebrations continued for three days.

Paris told Helen this story one evening when they were alone. She wanted to know more—she wanted to know everything. That's what usually happens when a woman begins to fall in love. And so he talked about his city with its beautiful walls and its wide streets, about the loveliness of its women, and about his first love, a nymph who was skilled in both prophecy and medicine. When he left the nymph she wasn't bitter, but told him that he should seek her out if he was ever seriously wounded, because she was the only one who could save his life.

"She must have loved you very much," Helen said. "How could you leave her?"

He shrugged, as if the matter was no concern of his, then changed his mind.

"It's not easy to love someone who's immortal. Someone who never ages, someone who is never in pain, when you know that you yourself will one day die and be replaced by others, when you watch your body begin to shrink, when you lose your hair, your strength, your desire. I wanted a woman who would age along with me, who would lose me, or I would lose her. Love without pain is nothing."

That was what he said, and that night Helen slept badly. She had a good marriage with Menelaus, and she wasn't unhappy in Sparta, but the gentle, melancholy expression in Paris's eyes had aroused something within her: the dream of a different life, away from the dusty roads of Sparta, away from the sharp, challenging eyes of the Spartans. Away from her husband's silence. Menelaus never spoke unless it was absolutely necessary. He saved his tender, quiet words of love for his war horses.

To put it simply, she was in love. It was wonderful. When she saw Paris, hundreds of butterflies danced in her breast. Her husband—whom she had chosen herself—was stronger than most men, but he had been raised to wage war, not to sit up late whispering softly to her.

Who could blame her?

Who could blame Paris?

Evening after evening they were together. One thing led to another, and one fine day Helen took a considerable portion of her generous dowry and ran away with Paris.

That was the beginning of a war that would last ten years.

The lovers' crime was not insignificant. The Achaean kings, with Agamemnon at their head, had sworn that they would support Helen's chosen husband. Menelaus wanted his wife back, and he wanted to punish the man who had stolen her away. He believed that Paris had forced Helen to go with him; he couldn't imagine that she would desire another man.

The conflict began badly. The Achaean fleet had gathered in the harbor of the small town of Aulis, but there wasn't a breath of wind; not so much as a leaf moved for months. The Achaeans sacrificed one bull after another, and countless sheep; they begged and prayed for wind, but their sails drooped like a donkey's ears. Eventually they turned to Calchas, the old seer. His advice was simple: Agamemnon must sacrifice his beloved daughter Iphigenia. However, he refused, incurring the wrath of the others, especially Odysseus and Menelaus: "Are we going to be stuck here for years, just for the sake of a little girl?"

Agamemnon gave in and asked Iphigenia to come to Aulis on the pretext that she was to be betrothed to

Achilles, the greatest of all heroes. It's easy to imagine how the sixteen-year-old's heart skipped a beat when she heard the news. All the girls dreamed of that well-built, fair-haired young man; according to the rumors, he was the son of a sea goddess. Iphigenia suspected nothing. The journey from Mycenae to Aulis took a couple of weeks, which she spent dreaming of the life that awaited her. And it's equally easy to imagine how devastated she must have been when her father laid her on the sacrificial altar with his own hands as he shed bitter tears.

"Why must I die, Father?" Iphigenia asked. Agamemnon's only answer was that sometimes it is necessary to sacrifice oneself for one's country, or one's honor for another person's honor; he could hear exactly how hollow those words sounded. They weren't just lies; they were a nauseating betrayal. And yet the girl must die. Then at last came the favorable winds that carried the Achaeans to the coast of Troy and the decade-long, desolate war.

Agamemnon paced back and forth in his tent, a nagging sense of unease filling his mind as he waited for the other kings and generals. They had trusted him so far—but for how much longer? Particularly after the spectacle of the previous day.

An old man in a white robe had turned up in the Achaean camp, carrying a golden staff. He brought valuable gifts of gold and cattle. He wasn't just anyone, he was the high priest from the temple of the sun god Apollo, up in the mountains. The men immediately flocked around him, knowing what this was about. Their commander, Agamemnon, had stolen away the high priest's daughter, Chryseis, the girl with the sparkling eyes. Over and over again her inconsolable father had pleaded with Agamemnon to set his daughter free. It was already ordained that she would one day become high priestess in Apollo's temple.

Agamemnon had always refused. Many of the men and their commanders thought this was wrong, an offense against the god, but they didn't dare to voice their opinions.

What would happen this time?

Would Agamemnon realize that not even a powerful king can oppose the will of the gods?

"You're a slow learner, old man. Why are you hanging around here?" he said.

The priest was no coward.

"Mighty Agamemnon, listen to me one last time. You can see all the gifts I have brought for you and your men. All I want is my child."

Agamemnon laughed.

"Unfortunately I want her too."

"But I also bring another great gift, one that cannot be seen. Apollo, the ruler of the sun, has promised you a great victory in this war, and a safe journey home."

The faces of the battle-weary troops lit up. May there be an end to this terrible war. May they return safe and well to their families. Even though they didn't say a word, their longing was so palpable that Agamemnon felt it rushing toward him like a warm wind. This made him even more angry. He had sacrificed his daughter to get to this war, but now he couldn't give up another girl in order to win it and to save many people from the darkness of death.

"Your daughter will come with me to my home, and she will grow old there. Until then she will work at the loom here and share my bed at night. Go away, old man, and don't let me see you again. If I do, not even your god will be able to protect you from my rage," he replied, as stubborn as a mule.

Everyone was horrified, especially Chryseis's unhappy father, who left the camp with tears in his eyes and walked slowly home beside the restless sea.

"Make them suffer for every one of my tears," he prayed to Apollo. And that's exactly what happened.

The army's already difficult situation became even more difficult. A merciless sun tormented them all day long, from early morning until late afternoon. The sea lay as still as a toad. Not a single ripple. It was also full of poisonous jellyfish. The men dared not bathe, and their food went bad very quickly in the searing heat. They were dirty, hungry, and tired. They barely had enough energy to put on their armor. They behaved like lost children during the daily battles, allowing themselves to be slaughtered like cattle.

Something had to be done, and Agamemnon was sum-moned to a council of war. When everyone had taken their seats, the Achaeans' greatest hero and warrior turned to Agamemnon.

"I think it's time to reconsider. The army can't hold out much longer. A plague has swept through the ranks, the men are suffering because of the strength of the bold Trojans and because of the fury of the gods. We must consult a seer or someone skilled in interpreting the flight of birds. What can we do to turn the fortunes of war to our advantage?"

After Achilles had spoken, he sat down. Calchas was also present; he was a well-known interpreter of the flight of birds, and he saw the future as clearly as he saw the past and present. He had led their swift warships through every danger and brought them safely to the green coast of Troy. He immediately rose to his feet.

"Achilles, favorite of the gods, you want me to tell you why Apollo is angry. I will do so, but you must promise to protect me, because I believe that the man who rules over us will be enraged."

"Speak up without fear, Calchas. I swear that as long as I live no Achaean will harm you, not even if you are thinking of the noblest among us," Achilles assured him.

Calchas then explained that the sun god was not angry because the Achaeans hadn't sacrificed enough bulls or sheep, but because Agamemnon had insulted his priest and the priest's daughter, who was designated to follow in her father's footsteps.

"If fair-haired, sparkling-eyed Chryseis is not returned to her father, the Achaeans will never win this war."

With those words he sat down, afraid that his legs might give way. Agamemnon's fury was not to be taken lightly. The mighty king shouted at Calchas, complaining that his prophecies were never in Agamemnon's favor, and this time was no exception. He was going to have to send Chryseis back. He paused for a moment, then went on: "Everyone knows that I prefer her to my wife, so why should I let her go? But I will do it, because above all I want what's best for the army. I will do it, but I want another woman to compensate for my loss."

"There are no more women," Achilles said.

"I don't care. I'll take Odysseus's woman—or yours."

That was too much for Achilles.

"You greedy wretch! I sailed here to defend your honor, and that of your brother. I have no quarrel with the Trojans; they haven't stolen my oxen or burned down my house. There are many seas and mountains between them and me. I came here anyway, and every day for your sake I face their heavy swords, their spears equipped with a sharp bronze spike, their deadly arrows. You will not touch Briseis, my woman."

Agamemnon laughed.

"I'll take her from your tent myself. Try and stop me, if you dare. I am the one with the greatest power; it was given to me by almighty Zeus, who gave you your strength. No one shall defy me, not even you. I don't care if you're related to the gods—or to at least one of them, since your mother left her door wide open day and night."

The other leaders held their breath. How would this end? Achilles placed a hand on his silver sword, but reconsidered.

"If you take my woman, you will never see me fight among the Achaeans again, and that is something you will bitterly regret. You yourself are as courageous as a roe deer; you send others to fight while you roll around in bed with your woman."

Agamemnon rose to his feet.

"Get out! You've been waiting for your chance. Everyone knows you're a good warrior, but you have a brain the size of a cockerel's."

Achilles drew his sword and took a step forward, but Nestor, the wise king of Pylos whose deep voice was like silken honey, moved between the two men.

"We have lost many comrades in this dreadful war; let us not attack one another on top of that. I am old and I have seen greater warriors and heroes than the two of you, but they listened to my advice."

Agamemnon had great respect for Nestor.

"You speak wisely, and I will do as you say, even though Achilles thinks he's better than the rest of us."

"That's not true, but I won't obey foolish orders. I promise not to fight for my Briseis, but woe betide you if you touch anything else that belongs to me," Achilles replied.

The storm abated.

Achilles returned with his people to his ships, while Agamemnon picked out twenty men, led by Odysseus, to return Chryseis to her father and the temple of Apollo.

He then sent two of his most trusted soldiers to fetch Briseis from Achilles's tent, and sacrificed one hundred goats and oxen in order to appease the sun god. The sky grew dark with the dense smoke, the men washed themselves in the sea then sat down to eat the animals' entrails.

The two men who had been ordered to collect Briseis walked slowly beside the gray sea. They were not happy about their task. They had no choice but to obey their king, even though he'd gone too far this time. The courage of Achilles was the only reason why the Achaeans hadn't lost this unjust war.

They found him sitting by his pitch-black ship and stood before him, not daring to say a word. He met them without anger in his heart; they were simple messengers, not responsible for their errand. His friend and brother-in-arms Patroclus brought out Briseis, the young woman who shared Achilles's bed. Admittedly she was his slave and he was her master, but they were young and beautiful, and a passion and an affection for each other had grown in their hearts. It was painful for them to be parted, anyone could see that. She accompanied the two men with heavy footsteps.

After a little while Achilles went off on his own, away from the eyes of his men, and wept—not just because

Agamemnon had insulted him, but because he had grown fond of Briseis with her night-dark eyes and her lovely cheeks. He hid his face in his hands and the tears flowed.

"Mother of mine, when you gave birth to me you knew that I was destined for a short life. In return Zeus promised me great glory. I am still young, but I have lost my honor. I have been kicked like a stray dog, robbed of my woman, whose caresses will now bring solace to my worst enemy. Never again will I fight in the midst of the battle; I will watch as the Trojans slaughter the Achaeans and I will not lift a finger until Agamemnon or his messenger begs me on bended knee to save them."

So he spoke, and eventually he fell asleep with a heavy heart.

———————————

Some of us had done the same—fallen asleep, I mean—but not all of us. My friend Dimitra had tears in her eyes. I edged closer to her. "Why are you crying?"

"I don't know," she replied quietly. It was an answer to think about; I wanted to console her, but I couldn't come up with anything to say. Our teacher took a deep breath, went over to the window, and peered up at the sky.

"Even in hell the weather can be good occasionally," she said, and sent us home.

As usual Dimitra and I wandered along together. It was a good opportunity to follow up on my question. It was one of those afternoons in the village when the sun leaned against the high mountains in the west like a weary shepherd leaning on his crook.

"Why were you so upset?" I asked Dimitra.

"Do you remember Katerina?" She was almost whispering, as if she were making some kind of obscene suggestion, and she had fresh tears in her eyes.

Indeed I did. Katerina was the village beauty, tall and slender as a cypress. Young men came from all over the area just to catch a glimpse of her. As she walked across the square to church on Sundays, every conversation fell silent. She could have had anyone she wanted, but her heart beat faster for a man she couldn't have because he was married. However, that didn't stop him from getting her pregnant. Her father couldn't bear such shame, nor could her mother. They lured Katerina to an isolated field, where they tied her to an ancient chestnut tree. Her father told her that he didn't want to do it, but he had no choice, for the sake of her three sisters. No man would think of marrying the sister of such a whore. No one could bear such shame. He shot her in the heart three times—once for each sister.

Then he and his wife went to the local police officer and told him what they'd done. Then came the silence.

The long, black, stubborn silence. Katerina was buried in that silence. Her lover emigrated to America, her father spent a couple of years in jail because there were mitigating circumstances involving the honor of the family. No one mentioned Katerina's name.

It really wasn't hard to understand why Dimitra was crying. Whatever happens, a woman always dies in the end.

Three

THE FOLLOWING DAY I was woken by the rain pattering on my windowpane. My heart leaped; the weather had been far too dry for far too long. The earth was thirsty.

On the way to school Dimitra said that our village might not be the prettiest in the world, but the smell of the ground after rain was so wonderful that the whole world felt like a caress.

Miss was already at her desk, and she had written on the blackboard in beautiful letters: *Ανάγκα και θεοί πείθονται.* Which means: Even the gods must obey necessity.

We were to write a short essay on this topic. We had absolutely no desire to do so; we wanted to hear the next part of the story about the heroes and the madmen.

Miss followed the example of the gods. She obeyed necessity and happily continued with her tale.

Agamemnon, pleased at having taught Achilles a lesson, slept much better that night. Toward morning his dreams became so vivid that he got up, put on his cloak and his sword, and went out.

It was a joy to the soul to see the first flush of dawn making the copper-clad ships in the bay glow like sunflowers. In addition, he was filled with conviction. The dream had been more than clear. It was an order from the highest power.

Without hesitation he instructed his messengers to call the other commanders to wise Nestor's tent. It didn't take long for them all to gather, tense and uneasy. What lay behind this unexpected summons?

When they were seated and had stopped whispering to one another, Agamemnon began to speak.

"Listen to me, my friends! Last night, during this immortal night, Zeus came to me. He had adopted your form, Nestor, and spoke with your silken honey voice, but he was very firm. 'Are you sleeping, Agamemnon?' he asked. 'You who are the son of the great horse-breaker Atreus and the commander of the long-haired Achaeans. Prepare for battle at once, for now the city of Troy with its wide streets will be taken; its fate is sealed. No deity shall prevent you.' I wanted to question him, to be sure that it was him and not some evil demon deceiving me while I was defenseless and sleeping, but he was gone. Therefore, let us all prepare our men for the final battle. But first I want to test them. I have the right to do so."

Agamemnon paused to see if there were objections, but no one spoke.

"I am going to tell the men to flee, and you, each and every one of you, must try to persuade them to stay."

What nonsense was this?

Wise old Nestor, who had ruled for longer than anyone on Pylos with its pale sandy shores, got to his feet and spoke calmly and thoughtfully, as always.

"If any other man came to us with such a suggestion and in such haste, we would certainly reject it. That is not the case here and now; Agamemnon is the most powerful among us. Therefore I say to you: Order your men to prepare for battle!"

With those words he set off for the tents housing his men. The others did the same; impressive men bearing royal scepters called upon their warriors, who poured from their tents and ships like swarms of bees. It took nine heralds to silence them so they could hear what Agamemnon had to say. He stepped forward holding his scepter, which in truth was the finest of them all. It had been fashioned with incomparable skill by Hephaestus himself, the lame god of craftsmen and the husband of Aphrodite, goddess of love.

"Listen to me my friends, brave warriors and vassals! In the past, almighty Zeus fooled me into believing that victory was ours. Today his message is different. He has ordered me to return home at once, and he leaves me no choice, even though the shame is great, and future generations will never understand how we failed to vanquish the Trojans, whose numbers are so much less than ours. If peace were declared right now and we sat down to eat and drink with them, and if every Trojan had ten of us to take care of, many of us would be left without sustenance. One of them to ten of us. Nine long years have passed, our ships are rotting, our anchors rusting. Our women and children have been waiting for us, and now we must return without having accomplished what we came here to do.

"So I say to you—and you must obey me: We are sailing home. We will never walk the wide streets of Troy."

At these words the men began to run back to their tents and ships, the dust whirling around them and forming a cloud over their longing for home.

The war could have ended on that day.

It was Odysseus who first made sure that didn't happen. He borrowed Agamemnon's scepter and ran from tent to tent, from ship to ship, exhorting the men to stay, not to give up now that victory and the sweet moment of vengeance were close.

"I understand that you are all longing to go home," he said, "but we will not return as wretched cowards, making our wives and children ashamed of us."

Wise old Nestor also played his part. He reminded them that Zeus had promised them victory but had never said it would be easy.

He added fuel to the fire. "You will avenge every groan, every sigh that faithless Helen's lover has heard. You will lie with the wives of the Trojans in their soft beds."

The men listened, and their lust for battle was reawakened. By the pale light of the late afternoon they could see the beautiful walls of Troy in the distance; they knew what treasures, what pleasures lay behind them. In addition, they wanted to see the most beautiful woman in the world: lovely Helen, lovelier than all their fantasies.

The Achaeans prepared for the final reckoning. Foot soldiers and horsemen from Sparta and Mycenae, from Argos and Thebes, from Cyprus and Crete—from every corner of Hellas, to put it briefly—were gathered. The powerful army moved forward slowly like a grass fire—and it was equally dangerous.

The Trojan lookouts on the hills surrounding the city realized what was going on and sounded the alarm. There was little time for discussion and deliberation. The king's son Hector, who was leading the defense of the city, ordered that the gates should be opened. Out came men, horses, and chariots at great speed. They took up their positions and waited for the storm while the elderly, both men and women, retreated to pray. The sound of their voices was like the hum of cicadas in an olive grove.

—————————

Miss paused at this point, and my friend Dimitra couldn't keep quiet.

"Miss, why were the Achaeans so cruel? Why did they want to go for the Trojans' wives and daughters?"

Miss held up her hands.

"Not to enjoy the women's favors but to humiliate their men. That's what they did back then, and that's what still happens today. A woman's body is the field of conflict where men crush one another's pride and honor."

"I am fourteen years old, and my body is not a field of conflict. My body is me."

Miss looked at Dimitra in surprise.

"I hope you never forget that," she said.

The rain was coming down more heavily now; it was as if the sky were a box being emptied over us. Suddenly a group of German soldiers ran into the schoolyard, stark-naked. They jumped around yelling and whooping, their fair-skinned penises swinging up and down and sideways. The Germans had been longing for rain too.

"The children are playing," Miss commented.

I didn't really care. I just wanted to touch her as she stood there with her long white throat.

"You call them children, Miss?" I asked.

At last she turned her gaze on me.

"I'm afraid so. That's what they are," she replied.

Her response was the only caress I got that day.

It was time to go home. Dimitra suddenly stopped beneath the mulberry tree in front of her house. We used to pelt each other with its ripe fruit when we were little.

"Promise me you'll never be as cruel as that," she said.

"I promise I'll never throw berries at you again."

She gave an exaggerated sigh. "I meant as cruel as the Achaeans, for goodness' sake!"

I caught a glimpse of Miss as we passed her house. She was standing at the window with her arms folded across her breast, as if she was trying to keep her heart in the right place. She looked small and lonely. Sometimes she would go for long walks across the fields and through the olive groves, her black skirt flapping. She moved fast, as if she were chasing someone or someone were chasing her.

It was impossible to tell.

Four

THE FOLLOWING DAY the sirens sounded again, although this time it was a little later. On this occasion the German battalion was ready, and their anti-aircraft guns forced the British pilots to stay higher up. The bombs were scattered at random, and we sought refuge in the cave once more. Without thinking about it we settled in the same places as before. Miss was smiling as she looked at us. I closed my left eye and pretended that her smile was directed only at me.

"So what shall we do today?" she teased us. She knew exactly what we wanted, and continued her story.

―――――――――

The Trojans rushed forward shrieking like cranes, a sound that could strike fear into the bravest heart. The Achaeans met them in complete silence, and this silence was even more terrifying.

Both armies moved rapidly across the plain, the dust whirling; they saw their opponents as if through a fog, but one man strode ahead of the Trojans. He was an impressive sight with a panther's head over his shoulders. He was carrying his bow and his sword, and in his right hand he held two copper-covered spears, challenging the Achaeans' leading fighters to deadly single combat. This was Paris, the man who had lured Helen from her husband's arms and home. The man who, more than any other, was responsible for this dreadful war.

The Achaeans were led by the betrayed spouse himself—Menelaus, King of Sparta. His long hair and beard covered his face, apart from his eyes. He made straight for Paris with such resolve that the younger man turned aside and sought refuge among his own.

Hector, son of Priam and brother of Paris, lost his temper and yelled at the lily-livered womanizer whose handsome face had brought such misery to the city of Troy and its people.

"You're afraid to face the man whose wife you stole? What kind of creature are you?" Hector shouted. Paris regretted his cowardice; he didn't want to look a fool in front of all the Trojans and Achaeans. He offered to face Menelaus man to man in single combat, but only on condition that the war would end, regardless of which of them won. No more deaths, no more widows and fatherless children—and Helen would go with the victor.

Hector and the Trojans thought this was a good suggestion.

Menelaus agreed. "We have all suffered enough because of something that really concerns only Paris and me. One of us must die, but the rest of you should make peace as soon as possible. Let us first make an offering to the gods and swear before them that we will keep this vow."

And so it was decided. Some of the men were sent to fetch sheep and oxen for the sacrifice. Both armies drove their spears into the dry ground and sat down, rejoicing at the thought of not having to fight anymore. The noise subsided, apart from the heartrending bleating of the sheep, who somehow sensed the fate awaiting them.

Inside the palace Helen was trying to suppress her anxiety by weaving a purple cloak when she received a visitor— one of Paris's sisters, the most beautiful, who came to tell her about the impending duel between Helen's lover and her former husband.

"You will belong to the victor, and the rest of us will be left in peace," she said. Helen felt a sudden sharp pain in her belly and doubled over.

"Are you with child?" her sister-in-law asked, her voice filled with happy anticipation.

Helen wasn't with child, but her belly was filled with longing for her former husband, with images of her own city of Sparta and her friends in their short dresses. Her eyes filled with tears when she thought of the olive and lemon groves, of the clear, swirling waters. She had left everything behind for the love of a stranger, but the memories had remained with her, living a life of their own within her heart.

"No, I'm not with child," she replied.

She put on a shimmering blue shawl and set off for the city wall, from which she would be able to see the impending fight. She didn't even know what she wanted, deep down. To be invisible, perhaps—the stranger's most frequent daydream. She knew that everyone's eyes were upon her.

Many had gathered to watch. The news of the encounter between Menelaus and Paris had proved an irresistible draw to those who were not capable of fighting—old men, women, small children. Helen felt as if they were all looking at her, blaming her. She was the one who had brought death and misfortune with her. She was the source of all evil.

However, she was wrong. The people appreciated her beauty, particularly the elderly, who sighed deeply as if they were watching yet another spring pass by, while they themselves were too weak to go along with it.

King Priam was seated on a flat area of the high wall, surrounded by his advisers. One of them whispered that it was worth going to war for a woman like that; we die only once. Helen's shawl gave a hint of her high bosom, her silken-soft skin.

Priam greeted her like a daughter.

"Come and sit by me. My son, your husband, is about to engage in a fight to the death. Who is his opponent? Is it the man who stands a head taller than all the rest, or the one who is a little shorter but has the chest and shoulders of a lion?"

"No, my king. The tall man is Agamemnon, ruler of many cities and a hardened warrior. The other is Odysseus, whose tongue is sharper than his sword."

"Can you see your former husband anywhere?"

"Yes—he is standing motionless, but that is misleading. He is as strong as an ox and as fierce as a tiger. He is at his most dangerous when standing still."

On the open plain below the walls, many sheep and oxen had been sacrificed. The smoke rose straight up into the sky, difficult to interpret. The two opponents stepped forward. Paris and Menelaus. Now the outcome of the war would be decided—and in whose bed Helen would wake the next morning. She was in love with Paris, while at the same time she missed Menelaus. She was happy in Paris's city with its beautiful walls and its wide streets, but she also loved Menelaus's Sparta, which had no walls apart from its men and women. She adored the blue-green sea below Troy, yet she longed for the river in Sparta.

She couldn't choose. She wanted everything. The gods never give anyone everything. She knew that. She closed her eyes as the two men began to walk toward each other, their spears at the ready.

There wasn't a sound in the cave; it was so quiet you could have heard a flea fart.

"So what happened?" Dimitra called out impatiently. Miss smiled.

"The next time the planes come, you'll find out," she said.

"I'll be wondering all night!" Dimitra said, which made Miss laugh. She didn't do that very often, and I was surprised. It seemed as if she didn't want to laugh. She covered her mouth with her hand as if she were trying to trap the laugh inside.

There were beads of sweat—like a pearl necklace—on her throat even though it wasn't the least bit warm inside the cave. She dabbed at her neck with a white handkerchief that smelled of lemons.

It was time to go home.

That afternoon Miss was going to visit a friend and colleague who lived in a nearby village.

We discovered that a bomb had hit the viaduct, which had been built by the Romans, and the windmill that had stood there forever. The sails were broken, no longer capable of turning.

"No point in the wind blowing now," Dimitra said.

Five

THE PLANES DIDN'T COME the following day, so we were supposed to have our lessons as usual. The visit to her friend had cheered Miss up, and she was wearing a red ribbon around her neck, which made her look like a peony. She attempted to explain Greek syntax to us, but the whole class wanted to know how the fight between Menelaus the betrayed husband and Paris the seducer had turned out.

She gave in, but it seemed to me that she was equally eager to continue with the story. She took a moment to prepare herself as usual, covering her face with her hands as if she were trying to hide from us, then immediately removing them and slowly reappearing like the moon from behind the clouds.

The time had come. Both the Trojans and the Achaeans had eaten their fill of the animals that had been sacrificed. Only

Paris and Menelaus had not partaken. They were standing to one side, surrounded by their closest companions, who were providing wise words and encouragement. "Paris is nothing without his bow," Odysseus said. "Menelaus is strong, but slow. Take him by surprise," Hector advised Paris.

And that was exactly what happened. Paris hurled his spear before Menelaus had even managed to swallow the saliva in his mouth. His well-made shield saved him, and he threw his own spear with strength fueled by anger. It went straight through Paris's shield, and its sharp point scratched the younger man's flesh. Menelaus leaped forward and attempted to bring down his heavy sword on Paris's crested helmet. At that moment something extraordinary happened. The sword broke in two. Menelaus couldn't believe his eyes, and in that brief moment Paris managed to get away. Menelaus searched for him, the Trojans searched for him, but he was famed for his ability to run, and he was already gone, on the way into the city and home.

Helen had also returned home. She reproached him bitterly for his cowardice and for his earlier boast that he was superior to her former husband in every way, both in the field of honor and in the double bed. Paris was crushed. He fell to his knees before her and begged her to let him explain. He wasn't a coward—it was just that he'd suddenly realized he could die. At that moment he was seized by such overwhelming desire for her that it clouded his mind. He wanted her like never before; he hadn't even felt this way the very first time they lay together. His entire body was trembling. He didn't want to die a hero, or in any other way, until he had held her in his arms for one last time.

Helen saw the tears on his cheeks, she saw the beautiful face that had made her leave her home and her husband and her newborn son, bringing unhappiness and shame upon herself. She remembered their first coupling as if it were yesterday. They had ridden for a whole day and night without stopping in order to get as far away from Sparta as possible. In the morning they reached a deserted inlet in the Bay of Corinth. Dawn was breaking. They dismounted and threw themselves at each other with a certainty she would never experience again. What had happened was inevitable. She was doomed to desire him. Even if he lied, even if he wasn't the man she'd thought he was. She forgave his cowardice and led him into the bedroom.

As the two of them lay in each other's arms, the search for Paris continued. The Trojans joined in because they wanted the war to end, not because they were concerned for Paris's welfare. Eventually Agamemnon spoke.

"Listen to me, Trojans and Achaeans! It is clear that Paris has run away from the fight, and therefore victory must go to Menelaus. I know my brother. Such a victory is a bitter blow for him. However, it is still a victory. It means that Helen must return to him with all the treasures she took from Sparta. An agreed sum must also be paid in reparation.

Then we will sail home and peace will reign between us, as we promised the gods with sacrifices and sacred oaths."

The men were tired of the war, and cheered to show their approval.

The gods were not happy. Nor was Menelaus. He wanted to see Paris lying dead on the dry ground, he wanted everyone to witness the deed and to remember that the act of taking another man's wife does not go unpunished.

He was standing a little way off angrily mulling things over when he suddenly felt a sharp pain in his stomach. A black arrow had pierced his coat and belt, and blood was pouring from the wound. Agamemnon ran to his injured brother.

"The Trojans have broken the truce. That will cost them dearly, but first we must take care of you," he said. It turned out that Menelaus wasn't as seriously hurt as they had first feared.

The Achaeans stormed across the plain, disgusted by the treachery of the Trojans, who were taken by surprise; they knew nothing of the arrow that had struck Menelaus. It took a while before they were able to muster resistance. They were also lacking their leader, Hector, who had taken advantage of the truce to go and see his wife and newborn son.

When he heard what had happened he wanted to rush straight back, but his wife, Andromache, begged him to stay, not to make her a widow and leave his son without a father.

"If I lose you, I lose everything," she said, and it was the truth. Her father and brothers had died in different wars, her mother and sisters were serving as slaves. She was the only one who was free and loved. She placed the child in his arms, but the boy was frightened by his father's crested helmet and burst into tears. Hector took off his helmet, consoled his son, and gently caressed his wife's cheek. She smiled at him, her eyes full of tears.

"Do not be sad, beloved. No one will kill me before my time comes," Hector reassured her. "But I know that time will come, as it will for everyone, the cowardly and the brave. Until then I must defend our city and our liberty. Nothing would cause me more pain than for you to end up enslaved in one of their beds. Go home with our son and let me do my duty."

Andromache held him tight and the warmth of her body gave him pause for a second or two before he freed himself from her embrace with great sorrow and tenderness, and set off to meet his fate. Paris followed close behind like a dog with its tail between its legs, determined to show that he was a better man than he had been so far.

The Trojans lost many a battle during the confusion of those first few hours, but the arrival of Hector and Paris gave them fresh strength, and they slew a large number of Achaeans. The conflict continued all day long. Many courageous men from both sides died the black death, the injured moaned in pain, and terrified, riderless horses galloped straight through the foot soldiers, causing even greater terror and havoc.

Little remained of the sun's light, night was approaching when Hector raised his long spear and held it up, parallel with the ground. It was the sign for his men to stop fighting. Agamemnon did the same, and the two commanders stood just a few feet apart, bloody, weary, and full of sorrow. Both had lost some of their best warriors and friends.

It was at that moment that Hector had an idea.

"Trojans and Achaeans—listen to what is weighing on my heart. We have broken the pact we made this morning. I suggest we consider it afresh. Either you conquer our city and we go under, or the victory is ours and you go under. The finest men from all over Hellas are here. Choose the very best among you to fight against me in single combat. If my opponent slays me, he may take my armor to his ship, but my dead body must be returned to the Trojans and their wives so that it can be burned upon a pyre. And if I prevail over my opponent, with the help of the sun god Apollo, then I will take his armor and hang it up in the holy temple, but his body will be returned to you for burial. You are welcome to build a monument in his honor by the Hellespont so that all who sail by can see it. They will write that this man, however brave he might have been, was slain by shining Hector, and thus my name will live forever."

Thus spoke Hector, and the silence that followed was as cold as the north wind. Many of the Achaeans were ashamed because they were afraid to accept the challenge, and injured Menelaus could not stop himself from insulting them.

"What are you—little girls?" he roared as he began to put on his armor in order to face Hector. It was sheer madness, and everyone knew it. Agamemnon did not mince his words.

"You have lost your mind, my brother. You cannot fight a great warrior like Hector when you're already hurt." Menelaus knew he was right, and sat down again.

Even wise old Nestor boasted that if he were not so advanced in years, he would happily go up against Hector. That hit home. Nine kings and Agamemnon, the supreme commander, volunteered. However, only one was needed, and the choice was made by drawing lots.

The man selected was Ajax, King of Salamis, who had sailed to Troy with twelve ships. He was a tall and handsome man, gentle in his ways but a lion in battle. Hector's face lost some of its color when Ajax stood opposite him, carrying a shield made from the hides of seven oxen covered in bronze plating, and a spear that was longer than any Hector had ever seen.

As was the custom, the two men exchanged insults in order to heighten the tension.

"You think you are great and mighty, Ajax, but what I see before me is a pile of shit with legs, hiding behind a big shield," Hector began.

"Keep on talking out of your backside for as long as you can," Ajax replied calmly, raising his throwing arm.

"The Achaean who is more powerful than me has not yet been born," Hector hissed, hurling his own spear first. It whistled through the air faster than a glance, it was impossible to evade it, and it pierced the bronze plating on Ajax's shield and six of the oxhides—but not the seventh, which had been strengthened with silver.

Ajax was more successful. His spear slid over Hector's shield and caught his neck. Dark red blood spurted out, and the Trojans held their breath while the Achaeans rejoiced prematurely. Hector was not seriously hurt. He picked up a stone and threw it at Ajax, who in turn cast an even bigger rock, which struck Hector's knee and made him double over with the pain. Ajax rushed forward with his great sword, ready to slay him, when by some miracle two heralds stepped in and stopped the duel, because it was night, and night must be obeyed.

The warriors were happy to have survived, and exchanged gifts to show their admiration for each other. Hector, who was the more eloquent of the two, said that they had fought like madmen, but that they were parting as friends.

He went home to Troy, where his father was waiting for him, together with his wife, accompanied by other women whose long dresses swept the ground.

Ajax was celebrated as a victor by his countrymen. Agamemnon sacrificed a bull, which was butchered and cooked over the fire; they ate until they could eat no more.

The battle did not recommence the following morning. Both sides wanted to bury their dead. The Trojans did so without songs of mourning; they burned the dead on pyres in silence.

The Achaeans, by contrast, marked their grief with speeches and sacrifices, keeping the ashes of the dead so that they could be taken home to their wives and children. It also happened that a number of cargo ships from the island of Lemnos arrived on the same day carrying hundreds of barrels of wine, which they traded for jewelry, oxhides, or slaves.

The Trojans also purchased wine, and that evening there were very few warriors who went to bed sober—if any.

That's the way it is. We love differently and we mourn differently.

———————

Miss took out her lemon-scented handkerchief and wiped her throat and the back of her neck.

"I think we should let them sleep now; tomorrow is another day," she said.

"That's not fair!" Dimitra called out.

It made no difference. We were sent home.

My father didn't touch alcohol. I had never seen him drunk.

"We drink the wine—it mustn't drink us," he would often say. Dimitra's father, on the other hand, couldn't stop pouring wine or ouzo down his throat until every bottle was empty. He never turned nasty, he just became very talkative and boastful.

"When my father drinks he becomes twice himself. Not someone else," Dimitra said.

We didn't feel like going home. We went and sat on the swing hanging from the mulberry tree. We swayed slowly back and forth. Dimitra's thigh was touching mine and I was really happy, even though I was in love with Miss.

"We love differently and we mourn differently," that was what she'd said.

She's probably right, I thought.

At that moment Dimitra's father appeared.

"I see our little turtledoves are perched in the tree," he said.

Dimitra went bright red. He really did look twice as big as he actually was. His gestures were expansive, and he took up half the road as he stood there rocking from one leg to the other.

"What did I tell you?" she whispered to me.

He positioned himself right in front of me and, with a certain amount of effort, managed to arrange his face into a serious, almost severe expression.

"You know how much I love my daughter!"

That was unexpected.

"I can guess, sir."

"Well then."

He didn't say another word. He set off toward his house and Dimitra followed him, imitating his unsteady gait. Her ponytail swung from side to side. Before she went indoors she turned and smiled at me. She had grown into such a lovely girl.

The evening had come. A star fell from the sky, but I didn't have time to make a wish. If I'd had time, I knew what my wish would have been.

Six

MY MOTHER WOKE ME early the next morning. She told me that my grandfather was sick, which came as no surprise. He'd lost a lot of weight recently, and no longer had the energy to eat, talk, and joke as he used to.

"Is he very sick?" I asked.

"He's eighty-two years old."

Which meant that he had eaten his bread. That the kingdom of the underworld awaited him.

My grandmother shared this view. His time was up.

He was lying in the old, creaky double bed.

"Ask for his blessing," my grandmother whispered.

I approached him very slowly. He smiled and winked at me.

"They think I'm going to die, but I have no intention of going anywhere. I want to see how this war ends."

He sounded exactly the same as he always did.

"Grandpa isn't going to die," I informed my mother and grandmother.

I hurried off to school, where Miss was ready to resume the story of the other war, the one between the Trojans and the Greeks, who were known as Achaeans back then. At that moment we heard the sirens and the roar of the planes once more. We reached the cave just as the bombs began to fall.

Miss was perfectly calm and collected.

"Let us continue," she said, and that was exactly what she did.

The Achaeans were well rested when they woke the following morning. They each ate a piece of bread, drank some wine, and prepared for the impending battle. The Trojans did the same. The sun had barely risen when the armies charged toward each other on the open plain. Shield against shield, sword against sword, spear against spear. Men who roared with elation as they slew their opponent, men who screamed with pain as they were slain. The ground was stained red. Seen from a great distance the conflict would have looked like an anthill; there was hardly any separation between one side and the other.

However, one man stood out. It was Hector, spreading death and destruction all around him with his spear, which was eleven ells in length—that's more than sixteen feet. No one could get near him. The Achaeans fatally wounded his charioteers, first one and then his replacement, but Hector continued on foot, nothing could halt his progress. The Achaeans were driven back toward their hollow ships.

The battle should have been resolved, but the weather changed in an instant from bright sunshine to darkness and wind. Heavy rain came pouring down. Hector had to break off, because he could no longer distinguish friend from foe. This sudden gloom was the salvation of the Achaeans. They withdrew behind the wooden wall protecting their ships and remained there, downcast and heartsick, all hope gone.

Hector addressed his men. He lamented the fact that early nightfall had prevented them from defeating the enemy once and for all, and burning their ships. However, they had still won a great victory. They would celebrate, but they must also remain alert so that the Achaeans didn't sneak past under cover of darkness.

And that was what the Trojans did. They unharnessed their sweating horses from their chariots and gave them food and water. They gathered wood and lit huge fires that spread their glow over a wide area. They washed the blood from their bodies and their armor in the cool, clear waters of the River Xanthos. Meanwhile people emerged from the city with oxen, sheep, bread, and wine.

The warriors spent the night on the plain, feeling a mixture of joy and sorrow. Almost all of them had lost someone. Hector thought of his youngest brother, who had died when an arrow pierced his heart. The young man's head had drooped like a poppy weighed down by its seed capsule in a shower of spring rain.

It was a quiet night. The fires burned, the horses rested by the chariots, and everyone waited for the first flush of dawn.

Agamemnon got no rest that night. His army's situation was more than worrying. Their ships were unguarded, their losses in the day's conflict were great, and he missed Achilles, the greatest warrior of them all. His behavior had been foolish to say the least. Why did he have to take Achilles's woman? He deeply regretted his actions. Something must be done. He sent his heralds to wake the other leaders, and one by one they came to his tent.

First of all, they agreed to the immediate formation of a unit to guard the ships, and this was done. The key question remained: How could they persuade Achilles to return to the fray? Agamemnon was willing to do almost anything to appease him—send Briseis back, ply him with generous gifts of gold and silver, make him the commander of seven cities, give him one of Agamemnon's own daughters as his wife.

Odysseus, Ajax, and Diomedes, who regarded themselves as friends of Achilles, offered to go and see him. Old Phoenix also accompanied them; he had known Achilles ever since he was a little boy.

They found Achilles outside his tent, playing his lyre and singing to his dearest friend Patroclus of the deeds of mighty warriors. It was as if the war no longer concerned him, and he greeted his comrades with joy, particularly old Phoenix. He provided them with meat, wine, and bread, and everything was just as it used to be. But not quite. Achilles brusquely dismissed Agamemnon's offer of reconciliation.

"He took away Briseis, whom I love. Now he wants to give her back to me and expects me to be grateful."

"He swears by the name of Zeus that he has never lain with her," Odysseus pointed out.

Achilles was not impressed.

"That old goat would lie with my dog just to get at me. He has always been given more than enough, but he wants it all. He can try that with the Trojans, but not with me," he said.

Phoenix tried to calm him.

"Only death is implacable, my son. Wise men—and you are wise—allow themselves to be moved if there is good reason to do so. Only you can save the Achaeans from being slaughtered like sheep. It is your duty to help them, and it is what your father would want."

Phoenix had been like a father to Achilles. He had played with him when he was small, comforted him when he hurt himself, even taught him to aim his little penis so that he didn't pee on his feet. Achilles loved this old man, but he was no longer a child.

"My duty is to live my life—nothing else," he said.

Agamemnon's emissaries left the tent with heavy hearts. Phoenix didn't go with them. Achilles's servants prepared a comfortable bed with oxhides and clean sheets, and the old man fell asleep almost right away.

Patroclus also retired with Iphis, his woman, given to him by Achilles.

Achilles himself couldn't sleep. He wasn't sure if he'd done the right thing. Was he really prepared to allow his countrymen to die by Hector's sword and spear? Agamemnon had certainly behaved like a greedy warmonger, but that wasn't the fault of anyone else. Achilles also knew that this wasn't the whole truth. He missed Briseis more than he was willing to admit. His bed felt like a coffin without her. She had never been easy to handle. In spite of the fact that she was his concubine, his property, she remained herself.

"You can tear me to pieces and throw me to the dogs, but you cannot force me to love you."

That was the first thing she had said to him as she stood before him with her long dark hair, looking him in the eye without fear. He had plundered her city, where her father was the priest; he had killed the man she was to marry and taken her with him as his slave. But Briseis was no slave, and he could see that. He could see freedom in her tall, slender body, in her confident gaze, in her fine clothes. He realized that she meant what she said, and for the first time in his life he capitulated in the face of a will stronger than his.

He let her be. Briseis was free, but she wasn't blind. She saw him swimming naked in the sea, she saw him playing like a little boy with his beloved Patroclus. She saw him in the evenings when he returned to his tent after the day's battles, covered in dust and blood. She poured him wine while other young women washed his body with slow movements, the same women who would later climb into his bed. The desire began to grow within her. One night she could no longer fight it, and it was she who climbed into his bed.

It turned out that he had been waiting for her.

There were no other women from then on. Briseis made his flinty heart open up like a sunflower at the first light of day. He missed her. Agamemnon had stolen her from him, and his bitter resentment at this insult filled his soul to overflowing. No, and no again! Agamemnon would have to fight his war without the assistance of Achilles.

At the same time, he was aware that his life would be short. That was why his mother had dressed him as a girl when he was a child and hidden him away from the world so that he would not have to fight in this war. She knew he would gain great honor but would also meet his death. He knew it too, but was still trying to avoid his fate.

Was that possible?

He remained awake, troubled by his thoughts, until Diomedia, a girl he had abducted from the island of Lesbos, crawled into his bed and lulled him to sleep like a baby.

Agamemnon was downcast when he heard that Achilles had refused to help. He sat there, silent and gloomy. Diomedes, one of the emissaries, tried to console him.

"We will fight without Achilles. He has always been stubborn, and our pleas have made him even more obstinate. We will fight without him, and you, Agamemnon, will be the greatest of the great tomorrow."

These words gave everyone fresh courage. They offered wine to the gods and returned to their camp to rest. But not Agamemnon. He was still worried about the ships. It wouldn't be difficult for Hector to send a small group of men to set them on fire. He recalled the commanders and they quickly formed a guard made up of seven groups with fifty men in each. Odysseus and Diomedes also decided to sneak into the Trojan camp to see if anything was afoot.

Hector had the same idea. He sent a volunteer into the Achaean camp to find out if the ships were under guard.

Unfortunately the three men bumped into one another in the middle of the night, clad in animal hides. The Trojan tried to flee, but he wasn't as quick as he thought, and it cost him his life.

Odysseus and Diomedes entered the Trojan camp without any problem. The men were all sleeping side by side in rows, with their spears stuck in the ground. A short distance away were two horses that aroused the Achaeans' admiration. They had never seen such fine white horses. Odysseus took it upon himself to steal them, while Diomedes silently slit the throats of twelve men sleeping nearby.

They were hailed as heroes when they returned to their own camp. They washed off the dust and sweat—and the blood, of course. They positioned themselves facing into the wind in order to dry off their clothes. The sea breeze calmed them.

"Is there anything more beautiful than the sea?" said Odysseus. He had spent his whole life on the island of Ithaca, and at that moment he longed to return there. He was tired of the slaughter, tired of the war. Killing men in their sleep was an abomination, but they had acquired two splendid horses. They celebrated this achievement with food and wine and sacrifices to the gods.

———————

There wasn't a sound in the cave. Miss looked at us with a weary smile.

"I can't go on any longer today. I had a late night with my friend yesterday," she said. She walked over to the mouth of the cave and gazed out. She stood there for a while between the light from outside and the darkness from inside; she seemed as if she might burst into flames at any moment.

"All clear. We can go home," she said eventually.

A bomb had hit the shoemaker's house, but he and his family had managed to get down to the cellar and were unhurt. His wife was beside herself with rage and despair, shaking her fist at the sky and cursing while her husband tried to calm her.

"We're still alive. Everything else can be fixed," he said.

"And what about the chickens?"

The bomb had destroyed the chicken coop too. However, it hadn't touched the airfield, or the two German planes that didn't even have time to take off.

After a while virtually the entire population of the village had gathered around the unfortunate family, bringing food and clothing. The mayor said they could stay with him for as long as necessary.

"We are not mice. We are human beings," he said.

There must be something special about being human, I thought, but I didn't know what it was.

Seven

THE FOLLOWING MORNING I woke up to find my mother standing in the kitchen, singing quietly. She hadn't done that since the Germans took my father away. One thing was clear: My grandfather hadn't died, otherwise she wouldn't be crooning to herself. I lay in my bed and listened; I recognized the song. It was a terrible ditty that everyone trotted out on every occasion, at the slightest provocation. At potluck suppers and family dinners, engagement parties and weddings. I'd even learned to play it on my father's mandolin. I lay there quietly humming the harmony.

> She shook the almond tree
> with her small hands.
> The white blossoms covered her back
> and hair, they filled her arms.
>
> I took them from the top of her head
> kissed her tenderly

and spoke these words
to her:

You foolish girl, why the hurry
to turn your hair white?
It will happen anyway.
You too will become an old lady with a stoop
and glasses, trying in vain
to remember this day.

My mother had a lovely voice and a great capacity for happiness. When I went into the kitchen she said exactly what I'd expected her to say: "Your grandfather made it through the night."

Dimitra and I ran to school, where Miss was ready to continue, a black ribbon around the white stem that was her neck.

————————————

The day dawned and the light spread slowly over both Trojans and Achaeans, all mortal men, most of them afraid of what was to come. They thought about their wives back home, about their children or their elderly parents. Would they ever see them again?

A few of them rejoiced; the field of battle was their natural habitat. Mighty Ajax put on his armor—the bronze greaves, the cuirass. From his left shoulder he slung his sword in its silver scabbard, and finally he picked up his shield, which covered his entire body and which only he was strong enough to carry. It hung from a silver chain, with a three-headed snake writhing around it. On his head he set his crested helmet. It would be needed before very long.

His men stood ready by the trench.

Hector's forces came toward them with Hector himself leading the way, carrying his round shield, as if he had nothing to fear. The smell of his son was still in his nostrils—the indescribable smell of a baby, along with the scent of Andromache, as palpable as her warm body. He would recognize that scent among a thousand others. He swallowed hard and raised his sword.

The two armies rushed at each other like waves rushing toward the rocks. Honors were even to begin with, and both sides lost many men and horses. It wasn't until the afternoon that the Achaeans gained the upper hand, not least thanks to Agamemnon, their supreme commander, who strode along mowing down his opponents like a farmer scything his wheat. He showed no mercy, not even when two inexperienced young men fell to their knees and begged for their lives. It is the first time we kill that is difficult. After that, it quickly becomes a habit.

The sun grew hotter. The dead and wounded were covered in red dust from the fertile ground. Terrified horses galloped around dragging dead warriors or charioteers behind them. A number of the injured from both sides had sought the shade of the lone fig tree in the middle of the plain, but there too they continued to kill one another. Others crawled on all fours in the direction of the river's cool waters. The air was filled with cries for help and screams of pain. Men slew and were slain. They wielded their swords and spears, hurled huge rocks.

Agamemnon was the greatest slayer of them all, cutting a swathe through his opponents in an unquenchable thirst for blood and yet more blood.

Hector realized that his forces could not go on. He ordered them to withdraw and seek refuge behind the beautiful walls of Troy. However, most of them ended up outside the huge gate, which no attacker had ever succeeded in breaching. It was as old as the city and the great oak that cast its shadow over it, which was why it was commonly known as the Gate of the Shadows.

Right there, with their nearest and dearest up on the wall exhorting them not to despair, everything changed. The fleeing Trojans gathered themselves, determined to ride out the fast-approaching storm and face Agamemnon, who seemed to be invincible. Two boys, brothers who were much loved by their mother and father, tried to stop him. They almost succeeded; one of them struck Agamemnon with his spear, but it did not pierce the soft flesh. Agamemnon shattered the boy's helmet with his heavy sword, splitting his head in two and spilling his brains. His brother managed to stab Agamemnon in the arm, just below the elbow, but this did not save him; he was slain by a vicious blow to the neck.

Blood poured from the wound in Agamemnon's arm, but the supreme commander of the Achaeans continued to fight until he was no longer bleeding. Then came the pain, a searing agony that made him call for his charioteer to take him to the hollow ships where the army physician was located. At the same time he exhorted his men not to give up, but the day had turned to the Trojans' advantage.

When Agamemnon left the field of battle, the men's appetite for conflict sank like a stone in a barrel of oil: a little slowly, but it sank. Hector was an experienced warrior and noticed it immediately. He leaped down from his chariot and raised his sharp spears in a victorious gesture.

"The leader of the Achaeans is gone," he shouted, giving the Trojans fresh courage to launch a counterattack. Even Paris appeared on top of the wall and caused considerable damage with his bow.

The Achaeans found it hard to resist without Agamemnon. The army became like an octopus: many tentacles and no head. Odysseus and Diomedes took Agamemnon's place, but Paris managed to shoot an arrow into Diomedes's foot, and was so happy that he broke into a defiant little dance.

Diomedes sneered at him. "Come closer if you dare, you stupid girl with your curly hair."

Paris was neither stupid nor a girl. He was already taking aim once more, but Odysseus covered his wounded comrade with his shield so that he could draw the arrow out of his foot. The blood spurted and the pain was unbearable. In spite of his boastful attitude Diomedes had to leave the battle and was driven away by his charioteer.

Odysseus was left alone and considered taking to his heels, but his legs refused to obey him. *They're not used to running away*, he thought, and soon he was surrounded by angry Trojans, like hounds wanting to tear a wild boar to pieces but lacking the courage to do so. Odysseus's reputation and his skill with the spear enabled him to fight them off until a pair of foolhardy brothers challenged him. They were not from Troy but had traveled there as allies, determined to win immortal honor for themselves, and what honor could be greater than bringing down cunning Odysseus?

They hadn't really thought it through. Odysseus mortally wounded one of them with his spear, but the other brother drove his own spear through Odysseus's shield and in between his ribs. The pain was intense and Odysseus dropped to his knees. However, he immediately realized that the wound was not fatal. His attacker knew that he had made a terrible error and turned to flee, but Odysseus thrust his spear into the brother's back with such force that the point came out on the other side. The young man ran for a few yards, but then fell down into black death. Odysseus too was in dire straits; it was only a matter of time before he went under, and he shouted for help as loudly as he could. He shouted three times and Menelaus heard him over the noise of the conflict. He and Ajax rushed to help their comrade. They found him at the last minute, just as his strength was fading. Ajax covered Menelaus with his enormous shield, enabling him to get Odysseus away. Then Ajax launched his attack on the Trojans, slaughtering all who stood in his path, men and horses, until the rest fled in terror.

Hector knew nothing of these developments. He was on the left flank by the river known as Scamander to some, Xanthos to others. He caused great damage and created havoc with his chariot and his spears. However, the Achaeans resisted until Paris once again demonstrated his skill with the bow by firing a triple-barbed shaft into the shoulder of Machaon, who was not only a fine warrior but also the army's physician. It would be a serious loss if the Trojans succeeded in capturing him. Wise Nestor took him up into his chariot and drove back to the camp with his customary skill.

Meanwhile Hector learned that things were going badly on the other front, where Ajax had the Trojans in retreat. He made his way there at speed, driving his chariot over the dead and wounded; the wheels and undercarriage were soon stained red. It was a sight that made the Achaeans falter. Hector attacked them with sword and spear, mowing down men to the right and to the left and bringing chaos and confusion. He avoided Ajax, and Ajax avoided him. For the first time Ajax felt fear; something in his heart made him draw back. The Trojans saw this, and rushed at him in full force. His seven-oxhide shield saved him, along with the other Achaeans who came to his rescue, even though Paris hit several of them with his poisoned arrows.

Ajax was afraid that Hector would set fire to the Achaeans' ships. That couldn't be allowed to happen. He stayed where he was, exhorting his comrades to follow suit, and the bitter battle continued throughout the afternoon.

Wise old Nestor conveyed Machaon the physician to the safety of his tent at high speed. The years had weakened him, but he could still drive a chariot better than most. Achilles, who was standing in the prow of his vessel, saw that the Achaeans were being forced back toward the sea. It would have been natural to be concerned, to feel sorry for them, but the anger over Agamemnon's insult still burned in his heart. He called to his friend Patroclus, who was sitting in his tent. This was the beginning of Patroclus's demise. He came out at once, always ready to please Achilles.

"It won't be long until the Achaeans are crowding around us, begging for help," Achilles said. He asked Patroclus to go and ask Nestor if the wounded man he had seen on his chariot was Machaon, the son of the great Asclepius.

Patroclus found the two men in Nestor's tent. A girl with pretty braided hair prepared drinks for them and placed a dish of bread and onions on the table. She mixed the wine with grated goat cheese and white barley meal.

Nestor, who was a friend of Patroclus's father, invited him to sit down, but Patroclus refused. Achilles was eager to hear how Machaon was.

Nestor was normally a mild-mannered individual, but this was too much for him.

"What does Achilles care about our troubles and our wounds? Is he waiting for the Trojans to set fire to our ships and slaughter us, one after the other?"

Patroclus couldn't help wondering the same thing. Nestor drank a little more, lamenting the fact that he was no longer young. He recalled the great deeds of his youth, and the girl with the pretty braided hair refilled his goblet. He took another drink, and then there was no stopping the old man's garrulousness.

Patroclus listened politely, glancing at the girl from time to time. Eventually Nestor got around to what he had been trying to say in the first place.

"I recall what your father said to you before you boarded Achilles's ship to sail to Troy and this loathsome war. 'Remember, my son,' he said, 'that Achilles may be nobler-born than you, but you are older. And he listens to you.' That was what he said, and that is what I say to you now. Talk to him. Perhaps you can persuade him to change his mind. If that doesn't happen, at least he can let you join the battle. If he lends you his armor, then the Trojans might believe it's him. Your men are rested, they can easily drive the exhausted Trojans back to their city, far away from our tents and ships."

So spoke wise old Nestor, sowing the seeds of doubt and anxiety in Patroclus's soul. On the way back to Achilles,

Patroclus bumped into another old friend, who came limping toward him with an arrow buried deep in his thigh. His body was drenched in sweat, and blood was pouring from the wound. Was this to be the fate of all Achaeans? To die far from their native land, to end up as carrion for dogs and vultures?

The injured man gave him no words of hope.

"All is lost," he said. "Our best men lie dead or wounded by spears, swords, or arrows. You cannot help them. But you can help me to pull out this arrow."

Patroclus was in a hurry to get to Achilles, but he couldn't leave the man in this state. He put his arm around his waist and half carried him to his tent, where he took a knife and cut out the shaft. He washed the wound with warm water and rubbed ground sea buckthorn on it. After a while the blood ceased flowing and the pain eased.

A short distance away, the battle raged on.

———————————

Miss sat down.

"I'm as hungry as a wolf," she said, which made us laugh. We'd seen her eating in the café—a sparrow ate more than she did. She would stare at her plate for a long time before taking her first bite with panic in her eyes. She would pop it into her mouth almost by chance, as if it didn't concern her at all. So we laughed at her and she didn't take offense, she joined in and laughed at herself.

Dimitra and I walked home together as usual.

"I don't like that Achilles," she announced.

To tell the truth, I didn't like him either.

"He seems pretty full of himself," I said. I didn't leave it there. "He's got a weird name too. I looked it up in my dad's encyclopedia at home, and apparently it means 'he who is in pain or anguish.'"

"Really?"

"Yes."

Dimitra shook her head, and her ponytail swung from side to side.

"Well, we'll soon find out what he does next," she said.

People were sitting outside the cafés in the square. A few of the German soldiers were there too. They'd been in our village for more than four years now. Some of us had learned a little German, some of the Germans had learned a little Greek. Even my mother knew how to say *Gute Nacht, mein Liebling*. It was a calm evening and the air was scented with thyme, oregano, and ouzo.

"We could be happy, both us and them," Dimitra said, as if she were talking to herself.

I couldn't be happy. My father was gone, my mother wept at night. My secret love for Miss burned in my breast. So I said nothing.

We parted outside Dimitra's house beneath the mulberry tree with a nagging feeling that we'd quarreled, even though we hadn't. I didn't want to go home. Hoping to catch a glimpse of Miss, I took a stroll past her house, which was tucked away behind the abattoir. I clambered up into a cypress tree where I was practically invisible. There were no lights in any of her windows, but she was standing at one of them, brushing her black hair with long strokes.

After a while she closed the window. I thought it was a shame that she was shutting herself in, and even more of a shame that she was shutting me out.

I went home. My mother had cooked potatoes in tomato sauce. We ate in silence for a while.

"Mom, do you think Dad will come back?"

She shrugged.

"Where else would he go?" she said.

Eight

THE FOLLOWING DAY was Sunday, so we didn't have to go to school. However, we did have to go to church. It was compulsory for all children. The Germans also celebrated mass in the barracks, led by the captain. According to the rumors, he was a devout Catholic. I didn't really know what that meant. We were part of the Greek Orthodox Church.

After the service people gathered in the square. The captain was sitting with the mayor, and Miss was there too. All at once something came over me. I went up to their table, apologized for disturbing them, and asked Miss what the difference was between Catholics and Orthodox. The mayor was about to box my ears for my insolence, but Miss stopped him.

"Catholics believe in the pope. Followers of the Orthodox church believe in God," she said nonchalantly. Then she leaned across and said something to the captain that made him laugh out loud. Miss actually spoke German; before the war she had studied in Heidelberg.

In the afternoon Mom and I went to visit my grandfather. He was feeling better and entertained me with stories from America. He had emigrated there when he was young, but he couldn't bear to live away from our village, so he came back.

"Life is here," he said. "The rest is nonsense."

"Have you ever been in love, Grandpa?"

"All the time—with my little Maria."

My grandmother.

"I might be in love too."

"I can understand that. Dimitra is a fine eel," he said, but then we had to change the subject because Mom and Grandma called us to the table.

"Come along, old man," Grandma said briskly. Grandpa gave me a wink and a wry smile, as if to say that being in love is sheer hell.

We had lentil soup; Grandma had let it simmer for more than eight hours, and the hard lentils melted in the mouth like mulberries. Mom took a glass of retsina with her parents, and it immediately went to her head.

"Where are you now, my beloved husband?" she said straight out into the air, hoping that my father was still somewhere, at least.

"Don't cry, Daughter," Grandma said. "Your husband is alive—I can feel it in my bones."

The advantage of people who are easily moved is that they are just as easily consoled.

Mom and I walked home hand in hand.

The darkness was deep but didn't weigh very much.

Somehow, and for no reason at all, we were happy. Mom smelled of lemons too, just like Miss.

Nine

THE NEXT MORNING Dimitra and I walked to school together. I wanted to cheer her up, and told her that she was "a fine eel," according to my grandfather.

It didn't cheer her up.

"You're an eel," she said.

Miss was smiling on this Monday morning.

"I don't suppose I need to ask what you'd like to do today?" she said, and went on with her story.

While Patroclus took care of his injured friend, the battle continued with undiminished intensity. Hector appeared to be invincible, and his men followed him as a swarm of bees follows its queen. The Achaeans were constantly pushed back, defeat seemed inevitable. Only two obstacles remained: first, the deep trench that the Achaeans had dug, and second, the high wooden wall protecting their ships. Hector wanted to storm their camp, but his swift horses refused to enter the dirty water in the trench or to jump over it.

At that moment Polydamas stepped forward. He was an experienced warrior, and Hector's childhood friend. He pointed out that it would be madness to force horses and chariots into the trench. If the Achaeans launched a coun- terattack, the Trojans would be caught like mice in a trap. It would be safer to leave the horses and chariots behind and cross on foot.

Hector was not only brave but wise, and he thanked Polydamas for his advice. He leaped down from his chariot, and his men followed his example. He marshaled his troops into five companies, each led by a reliable commander.

However, there is always one foolhardy idiot who is determined to make a name for himself. A chieftain called Asius was in a hurry to gain honor and acclaim, and raced ahead in his chariot. Luck was with him at first. The Achaeans had left a gate in the wooden wall open in case any of their own had been left outside. Asius aimed for this gate, and his company did the same, assuming that they would meet no resistance. But the gate was guarded by two men who refused to give way, like an oak tree that does not bend in even the strongest winds, thanks to its extensive root system.

There was a fierce battle at the gate, and reinforcements quickly came to the aid of both sides. The Achaeans hurled huge rocks at the attacking Trojans. Many found their target, crushing helmets and crashing through shields. For almost ten years the Achaeans had laid siege to Troy; now all at once the Trojans were besieging them, which made the Achaeans fight with a fresh passion. The compulsion to defend ourselves is always stronger than the desire to conquer.

If anyone knew this better than the rest it was Hector, who had kept his city safe for all those long years, in spite of the fact that his forces were far fewer in number.

He remained on the other side of the trench, wondering whether to cross or not. Suddenly a black sea eagle flew across the battlefield from the left, with a writhing snake in its beak. The snake reared up and struck the eagle repeatedly on the breast, until the bird dropped its prey on the ground among the Trojans.

They had never seen such a creature before. It was blood-red, like fire. Nor was it afraid of them—quite the reverse. It raised its head and looked at them with an unfathomable expression, then slithered away and disappeared under a blackberry bush.

"It's an omen," someone said.

"It certainly is," someone else agreed.

"We need to call in a soothsayer who is experienced in interpreting such signs," suggested a third.

Once again Polydamas approached Hector.

"Everyone knows that a bird flying in from the left means misfortune. The gods are warning us. The most sensible course of action would be to turn for home and to be satisfied with what we have already achieved."

Hector had slain so many men that he was covered in blood from head to toe. He looked like death itself, but his heart hungered for even more slaughter.

"My dear Polydamas, you are talking like a cowardly old woman. You expect me to take notice of some passing bird?"

"It's a bad omen," Polydamas repeated.

Then Hector uttered the words that would reverberate through the centuries, long after he was gone.

"There is only one good omen: to fight for your country."

The first person to be fired up by these words was Hector himself, and he continued: "If any man refuses to follow me, I will kill him myself with this spear!" he said, exhorting his men to make one final, decisive attack.

They obeyed him, pouring down the hill like a raging torrent and hurling themselves over the wall. Their crested helmets shone in the rosy afternoon light, striking fear into the hearts of the Achaeans, who wanted to flee to their ships. They would have done so, if mighty Ajax hadn't stopped them.

They turned and threw thousands of stones at their assailants, who did the same. It looked as if the sky had shattered and was raining down on the conflict, so constant was the hail of missiles from defenders to attackers and vice versa.

Hector also received an unexpected boost. Sarpedon, a Lycian prince, appeared with his bronze shield and his long spears and entered the fight like a starving mountain lion who had spotted a herd of grazing cattle.

He was the one who managed to open the way for the rest. Hector smashed the lock on the gate with a heavy rock. Many men were killed on both sides. The Achaeans were fighting for their lives now.

There was no stopping Hector. Not even a god could slow him down as he pushed forward with his twin spears, his eyes as black as the night.

Eventually the Achaeans gave up and began to run toward their swift ships in a state of total disarray. But Ajax, the son of Telamon of Salamis, would never yield to a mortal who had been raised on bread. His namesake Ajax, the son of Oileus of Lokroi, also stood firm. The first of these two was big and strong as an ox. The second was small and quick as a wasp. The first fought with spear and sword, the second mostly with his bow and a shield so light that it didn't stop him from using his speedy legs.

Together they managed to inject fresh courage into the fleeing Achaeans, who turned and stood shoulder to shoulder, facing the onslaught of Hector and his men.

Things didn't go quite as easily as Hector had expected. He was beaten back, and lost several of his best men, who fell to either the spear of one Ajax or the bow of the other, whose arrows rarely missed their target. Any warrior who exposed the tiniest patch of skin for even a second immediately fell victim to his triple-barbed shaft.

Unfortunately Ajax the small also displayed his godless-ness. He cut off the head of a man who was married to one of Hector's sisters and threw it at the attacking Trojans as if it were a rock. They stopped dead when they saw the gory projectile flying through the air before dropping at Hector's feet. For a moment Hector was seized by fear as the head stared at him with open eyes devoid of light and life, but it wasn't long before he was filled by an even greater rage. He entered the fray once more, but without success and with fresh losses.

The situation was even worse for the Trojans on the left flank. They had the misfortune to encounter the Cretan king Idomeneus with his bronze-clad spears and his shield, which nothing could penetrate.

Many Trojans lost their lives there and met black death. One man's head was cloven in two, one had his belly pierced by a triple-barbed shaft, one lay with his intestines spilling into the dust.

The aim was also to take the armor of the dead to keep in reserve, and the struggles for this armor and for the body itself became increasingly bitter. Just as many men died defending the dead as the living.

They fought on, slaying and being slain, rushing ahead like gusts of wind, none of them prepared to give up. Even the wounded Menelaus rose from his bed and joined in. After all, it was for his honor that the Achaeans were battling and dying. It was for Helen's sake that so many had left their homes and families. Menelaus was still in pain, but he picked up his great spear and left his tent, and the Achaeans gained fresh strength when they saw him.

Helenus, the brother of Hector and an incomparable bowman, saw Menelaus coming—and Menelaus saw him. Both men acted simultaneously, one throwing his spear, the other firing off his arrow. Both missiles hit their mark. The arrow struck Menelaus's breastplate, the spear Helenus's arm. The arrow glanced off but the spear caused significant damage, and Helenus was forced to withdraw.

Menelaus had no time to enjoy this small victory. Instead he had to defend himself against the next assailant, a Trojan chief who was known to him and who was approaching with speed and determination. Menelaus let fly his spear a fraction too soon and missed, while the other man's spear hit the center of his shield. Fortunately it didn't go through, and the shaft broke.

And so they stood there face-to-face, sweating and out of breath. Menelaus drew his silver-studded sword, his opponent a bronze ax with a shaft of ancient olive wood, as hard as stone. The Trojan struck first and caught the ridge of Menelaus's crested helmet. Everything went black, but the blade hadn't broken the helmet. A blow from Menelaus's sword, however, fell on the other man's forehead at the base of the nose, shattering the bone. His eyeballs burst from their sockets and dropped to the ground like the marbles children play with, and he doubled over and fell where he stood.

Menelaus placed his foot on the dead man's chest, plundered his armor, then turned to the Trojans, using the corpse as a podium.

"Listen to me, you pathetic cowards! You who have insulted not only me by stealing away my wife, but also the laws of hospitality! You think you can set fire to our ships and slaughter us all, but however much you may dream of that, it will never happen. Because the all-powerful god, he who gathers the clouds in the sky, father of all of us, has favored you for long enough, but you never grow tired of the conflict as men usually do. When they are sleeping and making love, when they are singing and dancing—but you never tire of the war."

As Menelaus finished speaking, a spear struck his shield. The young man who had thrown it immediately turned and ran, but was caught by an arrow from behind. It pierced his bladder and he died in his comrades' arms.

And so the long day continued. The noise of the battle rose to the skies. At one moment the Trojans rejoiced, at the next the Achaeans, but neither side could be certain of victory.

Hector had been informed that things were not going well for his troops down by the ships, and he rode across the plain to give them his support. He saw many of his friends lying dead, while others were seriously wounded and were being conveyed back to the city. There he also met his brother Paris, the handsome womanizer and seducer of Helen.

"Where are all my friends?" Hector cried out in despair.

Paris might have had an eye for the ladies, but he wasn't a bad warrior. However, he was a simple fighter, not a shepherd of men like Hector, not a leader who could persuade those fleeing in terror to stop. He wasn't capable of turning a defeat into a victory.

Hector was more than capable. He led the way with his round shield and his crested helmet, which frightened the Achaeans just as much as it had frightened his little boy. The Trojans followed him, as one wave follows another in a stormy sea.

The Achaeans stood firm, as the cliffs on the shoreline stand firm against the surging waters, particularly when they saw a golden eagle flying high on their right-hand side—a very good omen. Both sides let out loud warrior-like cries and yelled insults at one another. Ajax sneered at Hector for remaining in his chariot, while Hector called Ajax a miserable wretch whose fat would soon be feeding the dogs. The two men clashed, shield to shield, sword to sword, spear to spear, and the racket filled the skies above them.

But inside the city, behind the well-built walls, the women wept as they received the wounded bodies of their men. Mothers and wives and sisters, and right in the middle of them all was Helen, the cause of this war.

Who would want to change places with me? she thought. She was ready to cut her hair, mutilate her breasts, lacerate her lily-white thighs with a sharp knife if that would be of any use or make anyone feel better.

She was going to lose either her son's father or her lover, either Sparta or Troy, either her country or her lover's country.

Whoever won the war, Helen would still end up the loser.

———————————

Miss's voice broke. Something in her throat or maybe in her heart made her fall silent. She slumped down onto the chair.

"I don't think I can do any more today," she said.

I ran off and fetched her a glass of water.

She gave me a nod of thanks. Like the rest of us I stood there waiting for those few sips of water to take effect.

Suddenly she gave a mocking smile.

"I felt so sorry for Helen, but I'm fine now. You can go," she said.

On that day Dimitra and I didn't head straight home. She had promised her mother that she would light the candles in the chapel outside the village, and asked if I wanted to go with her.

"Do you really believe in God?" I asked.

She didn't answer. I waited for a little while, then repeated the question.

Dimitra stopped and faced me, and I saw that her eyes were shining, as if she were about to cry.

"Sorry—I didn't mean to upset you."

She smiled and explained that it wasn't me who was upsetting her, but God.

I had nothing to say to that, and waited for her to go on. We were wandering along the desolate track leading to the chapel. The air was heavy with the aroma of the mastic trees, and we could hear the sound of running water.

"I do believe in God. I just don't believe he's kind or wise or good in any way. I get angry with him. Why are the Germans here? What are they doing here? Why am I a girl? I hate being a girl. I'll end up like my mother, with no education, married to someone who drinks and gets me pregnant twice a year."

"Things aren't that bad, are they?"

"Not yet."

We lit the candles quickly and went and sat on the bench outside the chapel. The whole village lay at our feet, with the fertile valley beyond. The world had a glow about it. Even the churchyard, filled with crosses and slender cypress trees, looked peaceful. Only the temporary airfield and the fuel depot were alien, but you could allow your eyes to slide over them, look without seeing them. They were there, but one day they would be gone. We knew that.

Dimitra sat by my side breathing calmly, surrounded by a soft scent. Her coal-black hair was the only dark element in the landscape. She didn't want to be a girl, but she was a girl, troubled by difficult questions.

"Do you believe in God?" she asked.

I'd thought about it. I'd been tormented by it. There was no avoiding the issue. Everyone in the village was a believer, or pretended to be. They all made the sign of the cross when they walked past a church. They all went to Sunday mass. But I wasn't a believer.

"No, I don't."

"Do you believe in anything at all?"

That was easier.

"Yes, I believe in you. I believe in Miss. In my parents. In people, to put it simply. Some are stupid, some are evil, but there's nothing else to believe in."

Cautiously I put my arm around her shoulders, and she didn't push me away.

"I like you," I said. "Even if you are a girl."

She turned and stared at me in surprise. Then she laughed for a long time, until she had tears in her eyes.

I couldn't understand why she was laughing.

Ten

IT HAD BECOME a habit now. Even those who had been reluctant or indifferent at first had capitulated. There weren't many of us—only seven in total. We were turning into a kind of village within the village, which had already awarded us the nickname "the Faithful Seven." Each morning we waited for Miss to continue with her story, and she didn't disappoint us. She arrived at school well before us and was waiting with shining eyes, as if we were about to celebrate her name day.

Were we all in love with her? I didn't know. But I was, and I woke up every day terrified that she wouldn't be there, that she would have gone back home. Seeing her was a miracle. I can't put it any other way. It was a miracle.

That day was no exception. She began to speak.

———————

Old King Nestor, whose name lives on in several languages to denote the wisdom that comes with age, was sitting in his tent drinking wine with Machaon, the wounded physician, as the sound of the battle came closer and closer. What was going on? Were the Achaeans being driven out into the sea?

"Stay here and rest. I will make sure you are given a warm bath; that will make you feel better," Nestor said to his friend. Then he picked up his shield of shining bronze and a spear with a sharp point, and left the tent.

Defeat was close. The Achaeans no longer had the strength to resist the Trojans, who were sure of victory. Nestor was considered to be the equal of the gods in terms of wisdom, but how could that wisdom help his country-men now? Should he join the fray? He was old and weary. Any Trojan stripling could bring him down. He decided to seek out Agamemnon, the supreme commander. There was no guarantee that he knew what the situation was; he had been injured and forced to withdraw from the conflict. It transpired that Agamemnon wasn't in fact resting; he was standing on the shore together with Diomedes and Odysseus—who were also injured—watching the battle with growing despair.

This was all his fault. He should never have insulted Achilles.

"Every Achaean must hate me," he said. "Hector is on the point of setting our ships on fire and destroying us. What are we going to do? Tell me, you who are wiser than anyone."

"The battle is not yet decided," Nestor replied. "The Achaeans are still holding their position. You three are wounded and cannot fight. We have to come up with something else."

Then Agamemnon explained his plan. It was very simple: to defend the ships at all costs, and to flee when night fell and the battle ceased.

Under normal circumstances Odysseus was a man who weighed his words with great care. He also frequently meant something other than what he actually said, but on this occasion he forgot his skills and shouted at Agamemnon.

"You idiot! You open your mouth and it's like frogs jumping out of a stinking bog! You are not fit to command these men, who learned at their mother's knee to endure the horrors of war. You are suggesting that we sneak away under the cover of night like rats leaving a sinking ship, forget that we came here to conquer the city of Troy with its wide streets and that we have suffered for almost ten years in order to achieve our goal. Do not say another word, because a king does not talk that way, a king who has received his scepter from the gods and who rules over all the Achaeans. Your plan is not only cowardly, it is also stupid. If the men out there realize that we're thinking of running away, they will lose their lust for the fight, they will start thinking about their wives back home, about the freshly washed sheets on their beds."

The color drained from Nestor's face. He was in no doubt that Agamemnon, who was known for his quick temper, would slay Odysseus on the spot. To his great surprise, the king stood motionless with his head bowed. He remained silent for a moment, then said, "I understand what you are saying, Odysseus, and your words have struck deep in my heart. You are right. I cannot order the Achaeans to flee. Neither they nor I would survive such shame. Have you any other ideas?"

Diomedes, who was the youngest and therefore hadn't spoken, raised his hand.

"We are not in the best situation. We three are wounded, and the army is without a leader. I think we should show ourselves; even if we can't fight, we can stand side by side with our men and give them courage."

This was a good suggestion, and they set off at once. Agamemnon led the way, thinking that Achilles would be satisfied now that his fellow Achaeans had either fallen in battle or were ready to retreat. They couldn't manage without him. *He's sitting there drinking sweet wine from Lesbos, waiting for me to come crawling, begging for his help. I will not give him that pleasure.*

Agamemnon grew more and more angry, until his whole breast was filled with rage and he couldn't breathe. He let out a yell, not as loudly as he could, but his entire body became a warlike roar.

The Achaeans heard him, and hurled themselves into the fray with fresh energy.

Even the Trojans within the city walls heard him. Helen recognized Agamemnon's voice—after all, he was married to her sister. *We are lost*, she thought. *When he roars like that, no one and nothing can stop him. That man sacrificed his beloved daughter for a favorable wind. He will not allow any of us to live.*

The Trojan army had the same thought, and continued to fight with the best motivation of all: the desire to avoid death.

The conflict became even more violent, because the Achaeans had to save their ships in order to be able to sail home, and the Trojans had to destroy them in order to save their city, with its beautiful walls and wide streets. They fought on the shore, the waves crashing into them. The sound of metal clashing with metal rose to the skies as the men's warlike cries grew louder and louder.

Hector was at the forefront, and was the first to hurl his spear at Ajax, the son of Telamon. It caught the center of the shield and Ajax took a step back, but he was still capable of picking up a huge rock and throwing it at Hector with all his might. The boulder struck Hector on the neck, and he spun around a couple of times before falling to the ground. He dropped his spear, and his heavy armor prevented him from moving. Several Achaeans rushed forward to finish him off with their spears, but they failed. Hector was immediately surrounded by the foremost Trojan warriors; they protected him with their shields and stood firm until they managed to convey him to his chariot, drawn by his swift horses.

When they reached the ford over the River Xanthos they stopped and bathed his body. He regained consciousness and dragged himself to his knees, but he vomited blood and collapsed again, with his eyes closed.

And then the slaughter began in earnest. The Trojans lost heart when their great leader was no longer present, while the Achaeans on the other hand thanked the gods and gained fresh strength. The shore was filled with lifeless bodies and those who were seriously wounded. Ajax, the son of Telamon, moved forward with his sword and spear, mowing down all in his path, while Ajax, the son of Oileus, deployed his bow to kill even more of those trying to flee.

It looked as if victory belonged to the Achaeans.

But it wasn't over yet.

Hector's comrades took him back to his home, where his wife, Andromache, was waiting with their little son in her arms. She'd seen worse. Hector was badly shaken, but he wasn't seriously wounded. This was probably the first time he'd met an opponent who was his equal.

"What is wrong with you, my dear husband? Will you be lying in your bed when the Achaeans storm our city? Will you watch as they force themselves on me and feed your son's soft limbs to the stray dogs?"

These were harsh words, and another man might have taken offense, but not Hector. He was proud and happy to have such a wife.

"Come and sit with me for a moment," he said. "I'm already feeling better. I will return to the battle very soon."

Andromache sat down, took his hand, and placed it on their son's cheek.

That was all Hector needed.

He had avoided death, and that must mean something. He got to his feet, put on his shining helmet, and he was Hector once more. He rejoined his men in the same chariot drawn by the same swift horses that had spirited him away. His wife's words were more powerful than healing herbs and plants. Proud and splendid as a young stallion he raced across the plain. His men let out a dreadful war cry and followed him. The Achaeans couldn't believe their eyes. They wondered if he was immortal, or if one of the gods was protecting him.

If you start thinking like that, you've already lost. With great difficulty a small chosen group stayed put in close formation to hold their position against Hector while the rest retreated toward the ships. But there was no stopping him.

"Let us burn their ships! I will personally kill anyone who hesitates and tries to run, and I will throw his body to the dogs!" Hector yelled, egging on his troops. They obeyed him, not only because they were afraid of him but because they were seized by the irresistible desire for revenge.

They rushed forward like a single body determined to drive the Achaeans to the sea, they tore down the wall as playful children destroy a sandcastle. Nothing could stop them, and nothing could stop Hector, who drove his chariot through the lines of the Achaeans, causing great confusion and even greater destruction with his bronze-clad spears.

The Achaeans gave way. They were pushed closer and closer to their hollow ships. Wise old Nestor raised his arms to heaven and called on the gods for help, but no help came from that direction.

As the battle went on, Patroclus, Achilles's closest friend, was sitting with the injured comrade he had met earlier. He washed his wounds and applied healing herbs. He was horrified when he saw the Trojans approaching the ships. This couldn't be allowed to happen. He couldn't hide away; he had to do something.

"I'll run over to Achilles and ask him to intervene. I know he's very bitter because Agamemnon took Briseis away from him, and I know he hasn't listened to anyone so far, but I'm his best friend. He might listen to me."

With these words Patroclus set off. Meanwhile, the battle intensified even more. The Achaeans succeeded in stopping the Trojans just a short distance away from the ships, but they couldn't drive them back even though they were greater in number. For their part, the Trojans failed to break through. A cousin of Hector's did manage to sneak past carrying a burning torch and was about to set one of the ships on fire, but Ajax, son of Telamon, spotted him and plunged his sword into the young man's breast. The torch fell from his hand and he went down. Hector saw it happen and threw his shining spear at Ajax, but missed. Instead the man next to Ajax was hit just below the ear and dropped dead on the fine sand. And so the battle continued. Contemptuous of death, the Trojans rushed toward the ships with burning torches in their hands, falling victim to the Achaeans' swords and spears, and above all to the arrows that rained down on them.

Both sides lost many good men. Neither was prepared to yield. Anyone looking at the field of battle from a distance might have thought that the two armies were dancing with each other. At one moment Hector and his men were leading the dance, at the next Ajax and his men. Back and forth, like the waves. It might even have looked beautiful. But only from a great distance.

At that point Miss stopped for the day. She looked tired, but at the same time more beautiful than ever. There was a glow about her that I hadn't seen before. A fire was burning within her, and Dimitra saw it too.

"She's in love," she said.

A fierce hope made my heart leap, but only for a second. I asked Dimitra how she could possibly know that, but she answered evasively, assuring me that everyone knew. I persisted and eventually she admitted that she'd heard her mother say so.

"Did she say who with?" I asked.

"No." Dimitra suddenly felt guilty for passing on gossip and refused to discuss the matter any further.

We parted at the mulberry tree without saying another word.

"What's the matter with you?" was the first thing my mother said when I got home. She always noticed everything about me. If a single strand of hair was missing from my head, she would notice. I didn't want to lie, so I didn't answer. I just went straight to my room, lay down on the bed, and thought about Miss. About the way her neck rose from her collar like a violet, and about her hands, which she moved constantly. Who kissed that lovely neck? Whom did she caress with those hands?

That's what I thought, and tears poured down my cheeks.

Eleven

THE FOLLOWING MORNING I waited for Dimitra beneath the mulberry tree. The branches were heavy with blossoms, and I could see there would be lots of berries. It was Dimitra's great-grandfather who had planted the tree, for the wide, cool shade it would one day provide. I would also like to create something like that. Something that will provide wide, cool shade for many years to come.

There was no sign of Dimitra, and I was lost in daydreams when she jumped on me from behind and covered my eyes with her hands, which smelled of lye.

That's how easy it is to cheer someone up.

I pulled one of her hands to my mouth and bit her palm.

"Don't tickle me," she said. Although she seemed to like it.

Miss was already in position.

As I said yesterday, Patroclus couldn't just sit and watch while his countrymen fought for their lives. He ran across the plain that the Achaeans had been forced to leave in order to defend their ships. He saw many of his friends and comrades lying dead—one with a spear in his breast, another with an arrow in his neck, others who had been decapitated or had their arms and legs chopped off. Some were still bleeding from mortal wounds. A few had still not given up but writhed in torment, begging for help, calling out to him as he hurried past, but there was nothing he could do for them—except in one case. He could not abandon his childhood friend Arion, lying there robbed of his armor, naked as a worm. His belly was open, his intestines hanging out, wriggling like snakes.

This wasn't the right moment to recall the sunny days of youth, or Arion's laughter; there was no time, yet that was exactly what was going through Patroclus's mind. He remembered their wrestling matches, which were in fact acts of love, their games in the rushing waters of the river.

"Help me," Arion groaned, "help me!" Patroclus drew his short close-combat sword and plunged it into his dying friend's heart.

"My greetings to Achilles." Those were Arion's last words, and they broke Patroclus. By the time he reached Achilles, the tears were pouring down his cheeks like a spring bursting forth from the rocks.

Achilles was surprised.

"Why are you crying like a little girl who wants to be carried, Patroclus? Tell me what's going on, and keep nothing from me."

So Patroclus came straight out and told him that the Achaeans were on the brink of defeat, and that many of their foremost warriors were either dead or wounded.

"You have to help them. I know you're angry, and I hope I will never feel such rage in my heart, but you cannot be so implacable. You cannot allow the Achaeans to go under. And if you feel unable to join the battle, if you are prevented by a sacred oath or prophecy, then let me help them. Let me wear your armor. The Trojans might think that I am you, and be afraid. And let me take a group of our men, the Myrmidons, who love a fight. They are rested, while our opponents must be very weary by now."

Poor Patroclus! He had no idea what he was asking, nor did Achilles, who was not prevented from joining the battle by any oath or prophecy. He was still suffering from the insult Agamemnon had delivered to him by taking away Briseis, whom Achilles loved.

He treated me like a worthless beggar!

That was true, but it wasn't the whole truth. He missed Briseis. He took other women to his bed, but none of them could help him to do what he needed the most: to forget who he was and the fate that awaited him. Many slaves found themselves in his arms; he belonged only in Briseis's arms, but she was gone. She was in Agamemnon's tent, spending her nights in Agamemnon's bed.

Achilles didn't mention any of this; he focused on the insult rather than the fact that he was missing Briseis. However, he didn't want to be petty.

"I can't carry this bitterness in my heart forever. I had intended to wait until the Trojans were threatening my ships, but now that they are upon the Achaeans like a dark cloud and our countrymen have the foaming waves at their backs, now that the whole of Troy has gathered at the city walls to rejoice, I am troubled. They would have fled at the mere sight of my helmet. Instead they are preparing to burn our ships and rob our countrymen of their means of escape. Take my armor and the Myrmidons. Drive the Trojans away from the ships, but do no more. The Achaeans must not believe that they can succeed without me. Do not attempt to storm the city. You and I will do that together. We two will open proud Troy's girdle."

As the two friends talked, Ajax was fighting a short distance away, utterly exhausted. Sweat poured down beneath his helmet, which had already been struck several times by arrows and spears and axes. His ears were filled with a roaring sound, and he could no longer see properly. His left arm was stiff from holding his shield, and he felt as if he would never be able to move it again. It was impossible to get enough air into his lungs, yet he refused to give ground. He held the Trojans at bay with his long spear in spite of their numbers, in spite of the fact that they were skillful and attacked him like angry wasps squabbling over freshly pressed grape must.

It was clear that Ajax wouldn't be able to resist forever, particularly when Hector struck at his spear with his heavy sword, leaving Ajax with nothing more than a useless wooden shaft. He had no choice but to withdraw as quickly as possible. At that point several Trojans rushed past with burning torches in their hands and hurled them at Ajax's ship, while others pushed their torches beneath it. The whole vessel was ablaze in seconds, the fire fed by the wind blowing in off the sea. Tall flames shot up like sails being hoisted.

Achilles saw what had happened. Ajax was his friend and comrade-in-arms. He told Patroclus to get ready, which he did as quickly as possible. He put on the silver greaves, then the breastplate that shone like the stars in the sky. Over his shoulder he hung the sword; he picked up the sturdy shield and placed the crested helmet on his head. Finally he chose two spears that sat well in his hand, but he did not take Achilles's spear, because he couldn't lift it.

Meanwhile Achilles's charioteer, a steadfast and courageous companion, had harnessed the two swift horses Xanthos and Balios, with the even swifter Pedasus in a side trace in case he should be needed.

Achilles had sailed to Troy with fifty ships, each one carrying fifty carefully selected warriors who were ready to follow him to their last breath. They were loyal, but they were not afraid to speak their minds. They had already criticized him for keeping them from the fray.

"Your mother must have nursed you with bile instead of milk, since you are so bitter just for the sake of some girl," a bearded giant had said to his face.

Achilles reminded them of their harsh words as he exhorted them to join the battle.

"The time has come to show you are capable of action too! The Trojans are here—they are waiting for you!"

The men cheered, then adopted their usual close formation, shoulder to shoulder. A newly fledged robin would barely have been able to fly between their lines. Patroclus and the charioteer took their place at the front; this was the most dangerous, the most vulnerable, and therefore the most honorable position.

Achilles looked at his friend in his borrowed armor. *That could have been me*, he thought, sending up a silent prayer to the gods. *Grant Patroclus your protection, give him glory on the battlefield and let him return alive and uninjured.* Then he stood at the entrance to his tent, which was in an elevated spot and provided an excellent viewing point.

The Myrmidons were an extraordinary race. As the name suggests, they originated from ants. Almighty Zeus had turned them into humans as companions for an illegitimate son, banished to a desert island by his wife, Hera. They also fought like ants, so close together that one man's shield also covered his neighbor's exposed throwing arm, the favorite target of bowmen. They had never lost a battle, and with Achilles at their head they were feared by everyone. The sight of the Myrmidons approaching with their short, rapid steps, their brown shields forming a carapace, was something few could contemplate without quaking in fear.

Patroclus led the way, exhorting them to honor their beloved commander who was not with them today, to win him yet another shining victory and to save the Achaeans from destruction. They marched forward like a dark cloud casting its vast shadow over a field of corn.

The Trojans were not lacking in bravery, even if they were shaken by the sudden appearance of Achilles—who was not Achilles—at the forefront of the Myrmidons.

This is how things were done in those days. First of all the commanders fought in single combat, one man against the other, without the intervention of anyone else. Only when one of them had fallen did the battle for his body and armor begin between the two opposing armies. Dying in the midst of the conflict was unfortunate, but being robbed of one's armor meant eternal humiliation.

And that's exactly what happened on this occasion. The two leaders drove at each other in their chariots. Patroclus hurled his spear first and struck his opponent on the shoulder, causing him to crash to the ground, whimpering. The Trojans scattered, and Patroclus was able to chase them away from the ship, giving his own men the opportunity to put out the fire. This was a great relief, just as when the wind blows away the thick morning mist and the world becomes visible once more, with its rivers and mountains and valleys.

The respite was short-lived, because the Trojans didn't turn and flee but fought for every yard they were driven back from the ships. However, the fortunes of war had changed. It seemed as if the Achaeans couldn't miss. Their spears hit necks, breasts, shoulders, stomachs. Everywhere. But it wasn't over yet. Cruel Ajax, the son of Oileus, captured a wounded Trojan chief. He should have helped him, according to good practice in war, but instead he killed his prisoner with a single blow of his sword to the throat.

Patroclus felled the men who stood in his way as an experienced lumberjack fells tall pines and small junipers with ease. Luck was on his side. But as I said, it wasn't over yet.

———————————

At that moment the sirens began to sound, and seconds later the first bomb exploded very close to our school. Two German planes took off to join the fray. We knew the pilots: One was called Wolfgang, the other Erich. Wolfgang was blond and handsome, and all the girls in the village stole glances at him when they thought no one was looking. Erich was short and dark. He was more like the local men, and the girls ignored him completely.

"Run to the cave," Miss shouted, and we did as we were told, but she stayed where she was, with her arms folded.

"Come on, Miss!" Dimitra shouted.

"I'll follow you in a minute," she replied.

But she didn't come.

The raid lasted only a few minutes. The British bomber dropped its deadly cargo at random, then sped away, protected by three fighter planes that kept Wolfgang and Erich at bay.

The sky was free once more, and we left the cave. Wolfgang and Erich were returning to the airfield. They flew low over us and waved. We waved back. However strange it sounds, we were on their side. They were our boys, defending our village. But Miss didn't wave. She was still standing there with her arms folded. She was smiling.

We settled down and she went on with her story.

Twelve

Hector realized that his men couldn't go on, and was about to give the order for everyone to withdraw behind the well-built walls of Troy when the Trojans received help from an unexpected quarter. Sarpedon, king of the neighboring country of Lycia, suddenly appeared; he was widely renowned for his skill with the chariot.

However, there was no stopping Patroclus. He continued to spread death all around him, including among Sarpedon's men, who fled even though their leader was desperately urging them to stand and fight. In order to give them courage, Sarpedon decided to take on the man who was causing such damage.

He leaped from his chariot, and Patroclus did the same. They were like two vultures, ready to tear each other to pieces with their beaks and talons.

Sarpedon threw first and missed Patroclus, but his spear struck the beautiful horse Pedasus, and the animal dropped to the ground, whinnying in agony. Sarpedon threw his second spear but missed again. The two men were very close now, both roaring, bodies drenched in sweat. Patroclus did not miss. His spear found its mark in Sarpedon's belly, close to his heart, and the king went down with a crash like a mighty oak. He continued to defend himself furiously against the Achaeans, who were determined to kill him and take his armor. At the same time he called to his allies for help.

"Do not let them take my body and my armor! If you do, it will be a source of shame and sorrow for all time."

He should have saved what little strength he had left. Death came down over his eyes as he spoke. Patroclus placed his foot on the king's broad chest and pulled out his spear, bringing the heart with it. He literally drew the life out of unfortunate Sarpedon, who would never return home to his fertile fields and gardens.

The battle could have ended there. It didn't. One of Sarpedon's men galloped away to speak to Hector.

"Do not allow the Myrmidons to defile my king's body! Our shame is great, our sorrow greater, but your honor too will be forever stained if you allow an ally to be treated in this way, a man who sacrificed his life for you even though he came from another land."

His words filled the Trojans with horror; they would never forgive themselves if they didn't take action. Hector immediately got to his feet to lead the counterattack, in spite of the fact that he was utterly exhausted.

It was still only early afternoon, but at that moment a dark cloud came over from Africa, and the drops of rain that fell were as red as blood.

The fighting grew even more savage and more difficult in the gathering gloom. It wasn't easy to distinguish between friend and enemy, and in the middle of it all lay Sarpedon's lifeless body, pierced with spears and arrows, covered in blood and dust. Patroclus had already taken his armor, and both the Trojans and the Achaeans swarmed around the corpse like buzzing flies. The Trojans briefly gained the upper hand. They managed to carry Sarpedon a short distance away from the conflict, they bathed the body in the waters of the river, anointed it with wine and scented oils, and buried it.

Once that was done they were satisfied, and lost their desire to go on fighting. Patroclus, on the other hand, felt invincible in Achilles's armor. Could it be his destiny to take Troy? To lead the Achaeans through the gates, put an end to the war once and for all? It was a dizzying thought, and it made him forget his promise to Achilles that he would not try to conquer the city even if it lay wide open to him, like his mother's arms. He even forgot that he wasn't Achilles, and ordered his charioteer to pursue the Trojans. They raced to the wall and Patroclus attempted to scale it, but he slipped; his sweaty hands found no purchase. Three times he tried and failed. He withdrew out of range of the bowmen.

Meanwhile Hector was standing at the Gate of the Shadows, unable to decide on the wisest course of action.

Should he go back into the city with all his men or risk one last counterattack? He thought about his wife and son. Shutting the gates of Troy would be the beginning of the end. The Achaeans would poison the water, the Trojans would run out of food, they would die a slow, agonizing death without the opportunity to fight.

There was only one option. He must return to the field of battle, but this time he would focus on one man, the man who had slain so many of his comrades, the man who was trying to take Troy alone. Whoever he was. Because the rumor had spread: It was not in fact Achilles but his beloved friend.

The decision made, Hector exhorted his troops to take up the fight once more, while he drove his chariot straight at Patroclus, who climbed down from his own chariot with his spear in his left hand, a sharp stone in his right. He threw the stone with all his might, striking Hector's charioteer between the eyes and shattering his brow bone. He fell from the chariot like a diver plunging into the sea.

Patroclus couldn't help mocking him, drunk with his own strength. He shouted, "You poor wretch—but what an acrobat you were!" He moved forward to plunder the dead man's armor, and Hector jumped down from his chariot and ran to the lifeless body. They stood on either side of the corpse like two hungry lions. Hector seized the head, Patroclus the feet, each determined not to let go.

Trojans and Achaeans soon gathered around them. The struggle was bitter and intense, with the charioteer lying there motionless, having forgotten everything about the art of driving a chariot. Man against man, sword against sword, spear against spear. Neither side was prepared to yield, and neither side gained the upper hand until late in the afternoon when the Trojans, who were far fewer in number, found themselves unable to go on. Even the strongest oxen must be released from the yoke when that time comes. The Achaeans dragged the corpse away and stripped it of its armor.

Once again Patroclus had the opportunity to remember his promise to Achilles; there was still time to return to his ship. But he kept on fighting, until his spear was shattered, a stone sent his helmet spinning to the ground, and he no longer had the strength to hold up his shield.

The Trojan warrior Euphorbus, known for his skill with the spear and for his prowess as a runner, immediately rushed forward and plunged his sharp weapon between Patroclus's shoulder blades, although this did not kill him. Hector drove his spear into Patroclus's stomach, twisting it around and enjoying the sight of the life draining from the man who had been responsible for so many deaths.

Hector couldn't resist speaking his mind.

"Patroclus, you dreamed of sacking Troy, of robbing its women of their freedom and taking them to your own country as slaves. You thought you could defeat me, but now you will feed the vultures and hyenas."

Patroclus sacrificed his last breath to respond.

"It will not be long until you yourself are dead, Hector," he said as death closed his eyes.

"That's enough for now," Miss said. "Tomorrow is another day."

I didn't walk home with Dimitra. She stayed behind, talking to a couple of friends, and I was going to play football. The village versus the Germans. It had become a tradition. That was the greatest mystery of all. One moment they were racketing around like evil demons, burning villages, torturing and executing people; the next they were playing football as if nothing had happened.

But would the match take place today, after the British bombs? The German captain wasn't easily scared. He was acting as referee, but the mayor also wanted us to play.

"Life must go on," he said.

And life went on.

We too were a mystery in my eyes. How could we? How could I? Why didn't I hate them wholeheartedly, why was I pleased when they praised my fair hair or my skillful left foot?

Is the need to love greater than the need to hate?

I had no one to talk to about such matters. Or maybe I did—Miss. One fine day she and I would sit down and talk about everything, but that day had not yet come.

As usual plenty of people turned up to watch the match. Miss was there along with her landlady, an elderly woman who was good at dealing with everything from cuts and bruises to broken bones. The Germans were crazy about her herbal remedies.

Needless to say the village was soundly beaten: 7–1. The German attack, led by Wolfgang and Erich, made mincemeat of our defense.

I was still happy. I had scored our only goal thanks to a lucky free kick from the twenty-yard line. The ball was heading straight for the goalie's arms when a sudden gust of wind made it change direction and land in the back of the net.

Afterward Wolfgang went over to the landlady and pointed to the back of his thigh. Miss looked on with interest, although she pretended not to.

Wolfgang went home with them to be treated. He was limping slightly, and Miss did her best to support him.

And the mystery grew: Is the need to love greater than the need to hate?

Thirteen

DIMITRA WAS WAITING FOR ME beneath the mulberry tree the next morning. This was unexpected; I was normally the one waiting for her. Ever since we were little. "Are you coming?" I would ask her. "Soon," she would reply, but it was never "soon," it was always much later. I was used to waiting for her. It was almost enjoyable. It gave my little life a certain meaning. *Waiting for Dimitra*, that's what I could call the story of my childhood.

"You were good," she said, "but Wolfgang's better."

Why did she have to bring him up?

"Yes, he is," I said sourly.

She noticed and gave me a push.

"Only joking."

I didn't really care. Wolfgang was better. My dream wasn't to be a footballer. I wanted to be like my father, or Miss. Become a teacher, read lots of books, maybe write one. That's what I thought, but I didn't say anything. It didn't matter. Having a dream wasn't part of the reality of life in my village. In fact it was downright dangerous. So I kept quiet. My mother used to say that I was "taken by the winds" when I sat opposite her in silence. She always wanted to know what I was thinking about.

I had no intention of telling Dimitra about my dreams either—the "fine eel" as my grandfather called her. Then all of a sudden she said, "I want to marry a poet, like Homer."

"But he was blind," I said.

She shrugged.

"So much the better."

When we arrived at school, Miss was standing by the classroom door, her eyes shining.

Fair-haired King Menelaus saw that Patroclus had fallen. The Trojans must be stopped at all costs from desecrating his body and taking his armor. Lowing like a cow determined to protect her calf, he rushed forward and positioned himself next to the dead man, holding his round shield over him. Everyone knew Menelaus was not to be trifled with, and his spear held off the Trojans. All except for one: Euphorbus, who had struck the blow that ultimately led to Patroclus's death.

"Step aside, Menelaus! Patroclus is dead, and I was the first to strike him. No one else even got close. Leave his body and his armor to me; I am owed that honor. Otherwise I will have to kill you as well."

Menelaus sighed.

"You arrogant wretch! Your brother was the same—he called me the most pathetic warrior of them all, which was why he didn't return home to his young wife. Not on his own two feet, at least. The same fate awaits you if you dare to challenge me. Listen to what I say and return to your men. Only fools learn too late."

The reminder of his brother's death failed to bring Euphorbus to his senses—quite the reverse, in fact.

"You will pay for his death, Menelaus. You will pay for making his young bride a widow who has to lie alone in her newly built apartments, and for bringing my parents such unbearable sorrow. Perhaps I will be able to provide some consolation when I lay your head and your armor at their feet. Enough talking. Let us see who will live and who will die."

With these words he thrust his spear at Menelaus's shield, but the tip simply glanced off. Menelaus's spear, however, pierced Euphorbus's throat and went right through his neck. He collapsed. His curly hair, held in place with threads of gold and silver, made him resemble an olive sapling in blossom, brought down by a storm.

Menelaus began to strip him of his armor, and he still looked so fierce that no Trojan dared to go near him. But not for long; in the distance Hector could be seen, approaching fast in his chariot. His crested helmet shone in the multicolored afternoon light, and his horses seemed to fly across the plain.

The sight made Menelaus's heart beat faster. He knew he couldn't take on Hector alone; he ought to flee, but he couldn't leave the dead man. What would his countrymen say? That Menelaus, King of Sparta, had run away like a feeble coward. He couldn't live with that.

Better to die with his honor intact than to live like a poltroon. Life is precious and he didn't want to die, but he stood his ground until the Trojans forced him to take a few steps back. He caught sight of Ajax, son of Telamon.

"Come here, Ajax, my old friend and brother-in-arms. We must defend Patroclus. We must carry his body to Achilles."

Ajax didn't need asking twice. He immediately ran to join Menelaus, carrying his long spear before him.

Hector had stripped Patroclus of his armor and was dragging the blood-drenched corpse behind him with the intention of severing the head and throwing it to the dogs, but when he saw Ajax he decided to make do with the armor. He dropped the body and returned to his chariot, which was being guarded by his own troops.

This did not go unnoticed by Glaucus, chief of the Lycians and an ally of Troy. He had already lost many men, including the peerless Sarpedon, whose desecrated body had been borne away by cheering Achaeans.

"What kind of man are you, Hector?" he shouted. "You look good, but in the field of battle you are nothing. You allowed your friend Sarpedon to end up in the hands of the Achaeans, you run away and leave us to defend your city, which is not our city. We are sacrificing ourselves for nothing. We are going home. If you had carried Patroclus to the square in Troy, we could have exchanged him for Sarpedon, but you dare not take on Ajax man to man. He is stronger than you, and that's all there is to it."

Hector swallowed his fury at this insult and answered calmly.

"How can you be so foolish, Glaucus? I am not afraid of the fight, but I have something else in mind. Come with me—together we will teach the Achaeans a lesson."

He exhorted his men to mount a fresh attack while he himself donned Achilles's armor, which Patroclus had been wearing. It was a perfect fit, as if it had been made for him. At the same time he was seized by sudden doubts. What if his own men thought he was Achilles? His own wife wouldn't recognize him right now. And yet he felt invincible in this new garb, his muscles swelling to fill every corner. His whole body felt bigger, as a sudden cloudburst turns a small stream into a raging torrent.

He gathered all his allies and neighbors and gave a short speech.

"It is not because I wanted your company that I asked you to leave your homes, but because I needed your help to defend the wives and children of Troy against the fierce Achaean hordes. That is why the city gave you generous gifts and provisions. In war one simple law applies: You live or die. Ajax, who is defending Patroclus's corpse, is not an easy man to take on, but whoever makes him yield and hand over the body to us will receive my helmet and my shield, and will share my glory. Let us go and do what must be done."

It was hard not to be inspired by Hector's words and by the sight of him in that magnificent armor, which made him look like the god of war. They began to move as one toward Ajax, who for the first time feared for his life and pleaded with Menelaus to call for reinforcements.

The fair-haired King of Sparta took a deep breath and yelled as loudly as he could: "Friends and comrades, all of you who have shared bread and wine with me, come and help so that Patroclus's body will not become a plaything for the dogs of Troy."

Ajax, the cruel son of Oileus, was the first to step up, followed by the others. Who can remember all those names?

The Trojans, led by Hector, launched a massive attack on the wall of shields that the Achaeans had erected around Patroclus. It sounded like the mighty waves pounding against the cliffs, the forward impetus every bit as strong as the withdrawal. First the Achaeans were pushed back a little way, but without any losses, and with the encouragement of Ajax, son of Telamon, they then succeeded in forcing the Trojans back. However, one of the Trojans had somehow fastened a leather strap around Patroclus's left ankle and tried to drag the corpse away.

Ajax saw what was happening and took immediate action. He brought his spear down on the man's head, splitting both helmet and skull in two like a ripe watermelon. The brains spilled out, as gray as ash. The man went down and life left him. He would never repay the pains his parents had taken in his upbringing.

And so they continued to slay and be slain. Hector hurled his spear at Ajax and missed, but his throw was not in vain. The weapon buried itself in the man behind Ajax, and he fell to the ground with his armor clanking.

It was a hot day with not a single cloud in the sky, except above that section of the plain where the battle for Patroclus's body was being played out. A short distance away beneath the burning sun the armies fought without interruption. Perspiration poured from beneath their helmets, spears slipped in their sweaty hands, weariness made their limbs feel numb, but they battled on.

Thanks to mighty Ajax the Achaeans gained the upper hand. He seemed to be unstoppable, and the men fled like terrified dogs before a crazed wild boar. Hector saw many of his relatives and friends mown down. This couldn't go on; perhaps it was time to bring the conflict to an end and return home, behind the well-built walls of Troy.

His friend Aeneas didn't agree. He was not a son of Troy; he had come to the city with his young son as a refugee after Achilles had laid waste to his own city and wounded him. He was not afraid of losing his life, and couldn't bear the thought of his boy ending up as the slave of some Achaean chief. To put it briefly, retreat was not an option as far as he was concerned.

"Hector, how shameful would it be to leave the field of battle conquered more by our own cowardice than by these brave Achaeans? Come, let us attack them before they manage to take Patroclus away!"

So spoke Aeneas, and Hector took note. If anyone was his equal, if anyone could match him in strength, skill, and courage, it was this refugee who was already facing the Achaeans, his spear at the ready.

Hector ordered a fresh attack and the battle raged on. Yet more men were wounded or killed, but who can remember their names? Over and over again the Trojans attacked the circle of Achaeans who had built a wall of shields around Patroclus. They did not retaliate, they simply stood there like a single bronze-plated body.

The dark cloud above them grew even darker, as if some god wanted to mark them out from everyone else. They were a small number of men, all of whom knew one another. They were beloved childhood friends or relatives.

It was a bitter and unrelenting struggle. The men were sweaty and covered in dust, bone-weary, but not one of them gave way. They were like a group of farmers pulling at a bull's hide drenched in olive oil in order to stretch it; each person pulls in his own direction until the oil is absorbed and the hide is ready. The Trojans fought to take Patroclus to their city, while the Achaeans were determined to return him to his ship. Neither side was prepared to cede, and so they continued to thrust at one another with their spears echoing against their shields, this copper sky.

There was only one man who did not participate in the tumult. Automedon, Patroclus's charioteer, remained a short distance away comforting the horses, who were inconsolable at the death of their master. They refused to move one more step, and stood by the ornate chariot with their heads drooping. They wept hot tears and their manes trailed on the blood-soaked ground. Automedon tried both threats and kind, gentle words, but to no avail. Suddenly something came over them; they tossed their heads and raced toward the battle. Automedon rejoiced and attacked the Trojans as a vulture attacks a flock of geese. However, he was unable to cause significant damage, because it was impossible to steer the chariot and to wield his spear or his sword at the same time. Eventually young fleet-footed Alcimedon leaped up onto the chariot from behind and took over the reins and the whip.

Hector had few weaknesses, but one of them was his love for beautiful horses, and these two were the swiftest and finest he had ever seen. They belonged to Achilles, and he wanted them. He was no more vain than anyone else, but his mind played tricks on him. He saw images of the citizens of Troy cheering as he rode in through the gates in Achilles's chariot, drawn by these two horses. Andromache would weep with joy over her husband. His son would inherit his immortal glory. He turned to Aeneas.

"Such horses should not be driven by bungling idiots. Let us take them," he said. Aeneas was more than willing to help, and two of their men joined in. Shields and spears at the ready, they ran toward the chariot, certain that they would meet little resistance.

They were mistaken. Automedon saw them coming, and although it would be wrong to say that he wasn't afraid, he was a man of courage. He had driven these horses for Achilles for many years. They had laid waste to armies and cities together, abducted girls, caused many parents to shed bitter tears over sons and daughters. Patroclus was not Achilles, but he was his best friend. Automedon was incapable of simply driving away; if he did that, his heart would break. He jumped down from the chariot and asked Alcimedon to stay close, so close that he could feel the horses' breath on the back of his neck as he waited, weighing the sharp spear in his hand. When Hector and his comrades came close enough, Automedon threw his spear with a strength he hadn't known he possessed, driving the weapon into the nearest warrior's belly. Just as when the farmer strikes the sinews behind the horns of an ox with a sharp ax, the man continued to move forward before falling on his back, the fatal spear swaying in his entrails as it followed the rhythm of his failing heart.

Hector also threw his spear, but Automedon jumped to the side and the point buried itself in the ground, where it quivered for some time.

Meanwhile more Achaeans joined the fray. Hector and Aeneas were heavily outnumbered and drew back.

Automedon stripped the armor from the dead man and felt as if he had avenged the death of Patroclus. It was a relief. He grabbed his spear, covering his hands with blood. He climbed back into the chariot to continue the tear-sodden battle, which became even more violent.

Fair-haired Menelaus was now among the Achaeans, and he appeared to have discovered fresh reserves of energy. His reputation as a warrior was not the best. This was unjust, and was more to do with the fact that Helen had left him. "A real woman does not leave a real man," the men muttered among themselves, and Menelaus was well aware of their thoughts. He also knew that Achilles would never forgive him if he allowed Patroclus's body to be defiled by the dogs of Troy beneath the beautiful walls of the city, and so he entered the fight with vigor, killing a friend and drinking partner of Hector's. He also managed to drag the dead body over to the Achaean side.

Hector felt great pain when he saw his friend fall to Menelaus's spear, and his agony increased as he watched the bloody body being hauled along the ground like a dead pig. The cloud above them suddenly darkened even more and a storm broke out. Lightning flashed across the low sky, terrifying the Achaeans, who interpreted this as a sign that the gods were against them. A brief hesitation was enough to give Hector and his men the advantage.

The Achaeans fled. It is not necessary to give an order in such a situation. Ajax and Menelaus could see what was happening. The Trojans' spears always hit their mark, while the Achaeans kept missing.

"We have to make a decision," Ajax said. "Do we attempt to take Patroclus's body with us, or do we make sure that we ourselves return safely to our ships, where our comrades are anxiously waiting? Whatever happens, we cannot continue to oppose Hector, who seems to have the gods on his side. Soon we will not be able to see anything. I would at least like to die in daylight."

As mighty Ajax lamented in this way there came a sudden gust of wind, almost like a sharp slap across the face. The sky cleared and the Achaeans' perilous situation became even more evident.

There was only one man who could save them. This man, however, this godlike warrior, was sulking like a three-year-old in his tent. He didn't know that his beloved friend Patroclus had been killed, and that his naked body would soon be tossed to the dogs of Troy.

Who was swift enough to warn him in time?

The best person for this errand was Antilochus, the son of wise old Nestor, who was renowned for being fleet of foot. Was he still alive? He was discovered fighting nearby, and wept when he heard that Patroclus was dead.

However, even if Achilles agreed to come to the aid of his countrymen, he wouldn't be able to do so right away—his armor was gone.

The most sensible option would be to withdraw and take their dead comrade with them. Menelaus and another man lifted the body and set off. The Trojans spotted them and attacked with warlike cries. Ajax and his men blocked their path.

"We never give up!" Ajax shouted. "We have lived with that reputation, and we will die with it." However, the combined forces of Hector and Aeneas proved too much. The troops around Ajax thinned out, many Achaeans died and others fled. Ajax fought on, and the two men carrying Patroclus's corpse plodded on toward their hollow ships.

———————————

Miss let out a long breath.

"I feel as if hairs are starting to grow on my tongue," she said. In other words, she couldn't go on any longer. Dimitra fetched her a glass of water.

It was time to go home for dinner. I was tired after the previous day's football match, and Dimitra was hoarse from cheering on the village team. She was also as happy as a lark for no apparent reason.

"What's the matter with you? Are you in love?" I asked. She laughed away my question, but at the same time her cheeks flushed bright red.

The square was busy. The mayor, the captain, and another officer we hadn't seen before were sitting outside the best café, guarded by two heavily armed soldiers. The three men were drinking ouzo and the captain was behaving deferentially toward the guest, who was not only older but clearly outranked him, and wore a large Iron Cross on his chest.

Dimitra's father saw us and beckoned us over to his table. For once he wasn't boozing but was cooling himself down with "a U-boat"—a lump of mastic resin in a glass of water. He knew what was going on: The guest was a major and was just passing through. Nothing to worry about.

We sat with him for a while. Miss passed by, setting off on one of her long walks in her heavy boots, with a military water bottle looped over her shoulder.

"She looks like a partisan," Dimitra's father muttered. That was a weird thing to say, but he had a point. There was something *decisive* about her.

Later on Dimitra's father ordered an ouzo, because he claimed that staying sober was starting to make him feel drunk.

Eventually the important guest got to his feet, shook hands with the mayor, and halfheartedly returned the captain's razor-sharp salute. He climbed into the passenger seat of a black open-topped Mercedes and sat there, straight-backed, as a guard on a motorcycle led the way, with another following behind. The small convoy was heading for the medieval town of Monemvasia, or Malvoisie as the French chevaliers dubbed it. He would spend the night there in one of the impressive fortresses, out of reach of the partisans, who had become increasingly active of late. He was also looking forward to dinner on the terrace high above the sea; the local delicacy was a fish known a barbouni, the striped red mullet. Pythagoras and his disciples did not eat this particular fish; they regarded it as unclean, because it was a bottom-feeder, finding its food on the seabed, which meant it inevitably consumed people who had drowned. The modern Greeks, however, loved its delicate aroma and soft flesh. So did the German major, and his mouth was already watering.

Then he was gone. The people in the square exhaled, and started gossiping as usual.

It was a mild evening, carrying the promise of a beautiful morning to come.

Fourteen

It was indeed a beautiful morning as Dimitra and I walked to school. Miss was waiting for us as always, and greeted each arrival with a theatrical bow. Soon we were all assembled, and she continued the story of a war that blind Homer had never seen, yet described more vividly than those who had been there.

Achilles didn't know that Patroclus was dead, but he began to worry when he saw the Achaeans deserting the field of battle, with Hector and his men at their heels. He looked anxiously for his friend, and his unease grew when he couldn't see any sign of him.

He sent up a silent prayer as he sat before the ships with their curved prows and sterns: *May the gods protect him, let not the Trojans rob him of the light of day.*

As soon as he saw Antilochus approaching with tears in his eyes, he knew that the worst had happened.

His dearest friend was dead.

The sun was so strong that its heat made a sound, like the muted vibration of cicadas far away. Suddenly Achilles couldn't see; he took the ashes from the previous night's fire and scattered them over his head. Tears poured down his contorted face. He threw himself on the ground, roaring in pain and pulling at his hair. His slaves, the poor girls he had snatched from their homes, ran over and tried to comfort him. Antilochus grasped his hands to prevent him from tearing at his own flesh.

Achilles was inconsolable. Why had he let his friend go into battle? He remembered the words his mother had said to him long, long ago: "One day you will lose the one you love most." That day had come.

How to find solace? He remained lying on the ground, the women weeping all around him—except for Iphis, daughter of the King of Skyros. Achilles had conquered the island, killed all the men, and taken the prettiest girls, including Iphis. He had given her to Patroclus as a gift. Iphis did not weep. She had done her weeping. From princess to slave, somewhere along the way she had run out of tears. She served Patroclus, crept into his bed at night; the human soul is a mystery. She grew fond of him, she even came to love him. So Iphis did not weep. She bent over Achilles, brushed the ashes from his hair, and whispered in his ear, "On your feet, Achilles. Your friend is dead, but you can defend his body, make sure it doesn't finish up in Troy, the city of the winds, where Hector will want to mount his head on a stake in the square. Do not let them mutilate him when he is on his way to the Underworld. You were the one who gave me to him. Now that he is dead, you must give him to me. I want to wash him, anoint his body with eucalyptus oil, I want to sing him all the laments I never had the chance to sing for my father, my mother, and my brothers, killed at your cruel hands."

Achilles was too deeply absorbed in his own grief to listen.

"My time on this earth has served no purpose," he wailed.

Meanwhile Hector fought on, filled with energy. Dressed in Achilles's armor he drove back the Achaeans as a burning torch drives back the darkness. The men bearing Patroclus's body could do no more. The Trojans attacked relentlessly with spears, swords, stones, arrows—anything that was capable of lacerating soft skin, splintering bone, crushing the skull. Three times Hector came close enough to grab the legs and try to drag the corpse away, but each time Ajax fought him off, even though he knew the final result was inevitable.

"On your feet, Achilles," Iphis said again. "Only show yourself and fear will strike the hearts of the Trojans."

But Achilles had no armor; Hector was wearing it.

"I can't go naked into battle," he said.

"That's exactly what you can do," Iphis insisted.

And Achilles stood up with tears in his eyes, ashes in his hair, and dirt all over his clothes. It was like watching the sun rise. There was a fierce glow about him that made the Trojans shade their eyes with their hands. At the same time he let out a grief-filled warlike roar that froze the blood in their veins. They saw him and they heard him, and that was more than enough. Chaos ensued as they desperately sought refuge, running from the battle like grazing sheep who have just heard the roar of a nearby lion.

This gave the Achaeans enough breathing space to carry Patroclus to safety and lay him on a bier. Comrades and friends gathered around him, deep in sorrow. Achilles joined them, weeping bitter tears once more when he saw his dearest friend lying there, brought down by a cruel spear. Patroclus's beautiful face had stiffened into a mask of pain and horror, and Achilles cursed himself for sending him away with a chariot and horses, not for a moment suspecting that he would never have the opportunity to welcome him back.

Night fell, necessitating a break in the fighting. The Achaeans needed all the rest they could get, and the Trojans also withdrew quickly. The situation was different now that Achilles had shown himself. They were tired and hungry, but they weren't thinking about rest or food. They had to decide on their strategy for the next phase of the battle.

Polydamas was almost like a brother to Hector. They were born on the same night and had grown up together. He was not as skilled with the spear, but he was much more adept with words.

"My friends, we must make a decision. Either we stay here, or we return to the city. If dawn finds us here, then we know what will happen now that Achilles is back at the head of the Achaeans. We don't have a chance. He will pursue us all the way to the city walls, where we will be forced to defend our women and children. However, if we return to our beloved Troy, we can be prepared if he chooses to attack. There, protected by our beautiful walls, we can teach him a lesson that even his horses will remember."

Hector couldn't believe his ears.

"Polydamas, my friend, I don't want to hear that kind of advice. Haven't you had enough of being under siege? Our city used to be acclaimed for its golden treasures; now we have sold everything to greedy dealers because the war costs so much. At last we have the chance to settle the score with the Achaeans once and for all. We will stay here, and at first light we will take up the battle close to their ships—not close to our city. Right now we will post sentries and eat our meal. Let me take care of Achilles. I will face him man to man, and we will see who wins. That is the rule of war, and it applies to everyone: Kill or be killed."

The Trojans cheered Hector's words, then sat down to eat. The matter was resolved, and it was time to rest.

The Achaeans, by contrast, spent the whole night keeping vigil over Patroclus. They spoke quietly of his virtues, his kind heart. They comforted one another, but Achilles remained inconsolable. He held his friend in his arms, howling like a lioness whose cub has been taken by heartless hunters. He was filled with regret as he recalled the promise he had made to Patroclus's father: that his son would return garlanded with glory after laying waste to the city of Troy. The gods had a different idea.

Achilles whispered into the dead man's deaf ear: "I know that my blood too will stain this earth red. My parents will not welcome me home either. But I will not lay you in the grave until I have taken the life of Hector, the man who took yours. And before your funeral pyre I will slit the throats of twelve young Trojans, innocent or otherwise, from the city's finest families. Meanwhile you shall lie by our ships where you can hear the sea, and your woman can go there and grieve for you."

Then Iphis came, self-possessed and dignified. Her hands trembled slightly as she washed away the congealed blood, but that was all. She anointed the body with oil and covered the wounds with sweet-smelling unguents. She also dripped a secret balsam into the nostrils to keep flies and other insects away. She dressed him in his white robe, then Achilles lifted his friend onto a bed and draped a linen cloth over him.

The men took up their hesitant conversation once more.

Iphis returned to her tent, walking along the shore in the darkness. It was a calm night. No wind, no crashing waves.

Suddenly she lost control. She sank to her knees weeping, pounding the still-warm sand with her small fists.

We sat motionless like flies stuck in honey. We wanted Miss to go on, we wanted to sit there in front of our Miss who had something *decisive* about her, but she was adamant.

"You must be patient—just like Homer. He didn't rush to the conclusion. We will follow his path."

That's what she said, and we just had to put up with it.

As usual Dimitra and I set off together. The square was crowded once again. The atmosphere was tense, and the German captain was sitting at a table with the mayor, who looked distressed. For the first time in ages the German soldiers were heavily armed.

Had something happened?

You could say that.

The German major had been killed in an ambush not far from the village near a very old bridge across the stream. It was the ideal spot. The bridge was so narrow that the major's open-topped car would have had to slow right down. He and his driver were killed instantly. His guards reacted with lightning speed; they had experienced this kind of thing before. They shot dead two resistance fighters, but the third managed to escape.

An investigation was now under way all over the area. It was the mayor's onerous duty to gather everyone in the square and explain what was going on. Anyone who had any information about the incident was to speak to the captain. If the perpetrator was caught during the course of the day, that would be the end of the matter. Otherwise, every twenty-four hours, three individuals selected at random from every village in the province would be executed.

People looked at one another. Did any of them know anything?

Miss was also there. She was just about the only woman in the village who, by virtue of her profession, could spend time among the men who were drinking ouzo and playing cards. She was sensible enough not to overuse this privilege; she would sit with the mayor and his sons on Sunday mornings, sipping cherry juice.

Dimitra was standing next to me, breathing faster and faster. I looked at her. There was panic in her eyes, and her mouth was half open as if she were trying to swallow air. I waved to Miss, and we took Dimitra to see Miss's landlady.

"I need to be alone with her," the old woman said. She took Dimitra to an inner room and closed the door.

Miss and I were on our own. My heart was pounding, while Miss seemed completely calm. She looked out of the window.

"The almond trees are in blossom," she said.

I had thought she was calm, but her eyes were sad and her lower lip was trembling as if she were about to cry. It hurt me to see her like that. There was nothing I could do. I was young, I was stupid, I was "taken by the winds," which was what people in our village said about someone who had ridiculous dreams. I was all of that, and for a moment I considered putting my arm around her, but I realized it would be the wrong thing to do. She would be surprised. She wouldn't regard me as a man, for the very simple reason that I wasn't one.

The door opened and the old woman came out.

"We can fix this," she said. "She's not sick, she's just frightened."

Dimitra was given something to drink, and fifteen minutes later she was herself again.

Miss and I stayed with her and talked reassuringly to her. Why was she so scared? Miss stroked her cheek and I stroked her hair. Then Miss allowed her hand to pass softly over mine, and almost distractedly she said, "Look after her."

It sounded so important, as if she were calling upon me to be a man. Dimitra had already lost a brother, the last time the Germans decided to execute people at random. Now there was a risk that she might lose her father. I tried to cheer her up by saying that the Germans were bound to find the guilty party.

"The guilty party?" she said. "Is there anyone who's not guilty?"

That night it was only babies who got any sleep in our village. You could see the lights on behind closed blinds. There was anguish in the air. I had no brothers to lose, I was my parents' only child. My father was already in a German jail, but I knew that the Germans were in the habit of executing prisoners whenever they encountered a setback. Was my father alive, or had he already been killed?

I thought about him, about my mother, about Dimitra. Most of all I thought about Miss. Her hand on mine. "Look after her," she had said about Dimitra. Slowly I understood that with these words she had been taking her leave of both of us. "It's you two who belong together"—that was what she had meant, without actually spelling it out. I wasn't an idiot. I knew that Miss would never be mine. And now it had been said.

It made me feel better.

Fifteen

MISS WASN'T STANDING at the door the next morning; she was sitting inside the classroom. She didn't normally do that, not unless she was telling her story or teaching us something else. She had opened the window, and the room was filled with the scent of almond blossoms.

Had something happened? Had the Germans tracked down the third partisan?

"We will not sit here in silence waiting for the barbarians. We will continue as usual," Miss said, and began.

———————

Dawn brought the light of day on her shoulders for both the gods and mortal men. Achilles had kept vigil over his dead friend and burned with the desire for revenge, but his armor was gone.

In the Achaean camp the rumor spread that he was ready to rejoin the fray, which lifted the men's spirits. Even

Agamemnon hastened to send him all the gifts he had promised to deliver: gold, women, and, above all, Briseis.

She didn't go up to Achilles, she didn't throw herself into his arms. Instead she dropped to her knees beside Patroclus's body, tears pouring down her cheeks.

"My dearest friend! You were alive when I was forced to leave this tent, and now you lie dead. Misfortune follows me wherever I go. Achilles sacked my city, killed my family and the man who was to be my husband, but you comforted me. 'Do not weep, Briseis,' you said. You promised that Achilles would make me his wife, that he would take me home to his city and marry me in front of all his warriors."

The other women wept too, more because of the fate that had befallen them than for Patroclus, but who can distinguish one sorrow from another? Who can distinguish tears from tears?

Achilles was done with weeping. He wanted to get out onto the battlefield right away, but the man who had killed his best friend was wearing his armor. How could he quickly find armor that was just as good?

It was Iphis who provided the solution. She hadn't slept since returning to her tent, but had spent all night working on Patroclus's armor. It might not have been as outstanding as the equipment Achilles had lost, but the shield was good, with images of a wedding between a goddess and a mortal man. The spear was long, with double barbs at the point. The breastplate was substantial, the sword sharp and heavy.

She polished each item with sand and water until the luster of the metal came through, as when the sun breaks through the clouds.

When her task was done she went and lay down on Patroclus's bed and curled up, just as she used to do when he was there. She could not rest. She had a plan. She heard Agamemnon's messenger arrive, she left the tent and heard what Briseis had to say. It was time.

She went up to Achilles and spoke to him.

"There is no point in grieving. It is better to spare your friend's soul the sound of your whining. Accept this armor, which only he has worn. He died in your armor. If the gods want you to die in his, then so be it. There can be no greater honor than to die for your friend."

These words were too much even for a hardened warrior who burned cities and villages without a second thought, slaughtered young and old, abducted young girls and gifted them to his friends. He was rarely alone in these exploits; Patroclus was almost always at his side in this armor. Putting it on would have been an act of sacrilege under normal circumstances, but now things were different.

Now he was going to bring his friend back to life, in a way. He tried the spear; it rested in his hand as if it had been made for him. He put on the breastplate and greaves—also a perfect fit. He picked up the shield; it was lighter than his but beautifully decorated. Finally he put on the helmet. It chafed a little at the temples, but that was all. He took a few steps, made some violent attacking maneuvers. The armor didn't impede his movement at all; quite the reverse. It felt as if it were part of him, like a sea eagle's wings.

"The two of you could have been twins," Iphis said.

"We were more than twins. We were one man. I trusted him more than I trust myself. If I died first he was going to take care of my son, my only son. All I want to do now is get started."

The rest of the Achaeans had also regained their lust for battle, and emerged from their tents and ships with shining eyes.

Achilles told his charioteer to harness the horses, then went and spoke to them.

"Do not let me down, Xanthos and Balios," he said. The horses looked at him with their big eyes, then lowered their heads.

Achilles climbed into his chariot and took his place at the head of the Achaean army.

The Trojans were also ready. Hector went from tent to tent, speaking to leaders and foot soldiers. The plan was to take the Achaeans by surprise early in the morning, which was why the Trojans were sleeping close to the ships rather than returning to the city, even though that was what they all wanted. To see their wives and children, their elderly parents. To say goodbye. No one could be sure they would survive the impending attack, not even Hector, who longed to hold Andromache in his arms and hear the laughter of his little boy. But they all stayed where they were.

The people in the city kept them company, albeit from a distance. They had placed large burning torches all around the top of the well-built walls. Old King Priam was seated just inside the Gate of the Shadows along with the other elderly citizens and the women and children.

Only Helen stayed away. She sat alone in her room, cursing herself for the misfortune she had brought upon these people and her own family. She didn't dare show herself in front of the women who were now widows, the children who had lost their fathers. Paris was the man who gave her pleasure, but he was not the one who made her proud. How could she love someone she despised? What was she doing here? She was a queen who had become a mistress.

These were the thoughts that kept her awake the night before the great battle. Toward morning she took a long bath, then dressed herself in a white ankle-length gown and gathered up her hair in a topknot, leaving her lily-white neck completely exposed. It was the first time she had done this, and there was an idea behind it, an idea she didn't really want to think through. But she had no choice. This was "the executioner's hairstyle"; the neck must be left clear when the head was chopped off. If the Achaeans won the war, that would be Helen's fate, and she knew it. In which case it was best to find out what she looked like with her hair up.

One last glance in the mirror, then she went to join the people in the square. Weren't they afraid? If the gods granted victory to the Achaeans, the men would be slain or sold into slavery, while the women would be raped in front of their children before being sold to traders from the islands, who would do whatever they wanted with them. All these people knew this, and yet she saw no fear in their eyes. Their hero was still alive, their Hector. The "shepherd of the people" was still alive.

Helen was an Achaean, of course; her sister was married to their commander, powerful Agamemnon. Two sisters, Clytemnestra and Helen, were married to two brothers, both great kings: Agamemnon in Mycenae with its impregnable acropolis, and Menelaus in Sparta, whose army had never been defeated.

Helen had humiliated them by running away with handsome Paris. If she had remained in Sparta they would have stoned her to death, or simply separated her head from her body if they wished to be merciful. There was a kind of shame that only blood could wash away, in their opinion. The Trojans were less harsh. Women enjoyed the same freedom as men. Andromache, Hector's wife, would often reassure her.

"We are women. The yearning of the heart comes first, and everything else comes second. No one here blames you," she would say.

"Men have a heart too, even if it is armed for war and revenge," Helen said.

Andromache was not a native of Troy either. Achilles had sacked her city, killed her father and her seven brothers. Hector had rescued her and married her, and now he was out there on the plain, ready to defend her life and freedom once again. She felt sorry for Helen. She couldn't foresee a happy outcome to this conflict; either Helen's former countrymen or her new ones would be destroyed.

And so the two women sat together, waiting.

In the distance they could see the armies moving toward each other in the early-morning light. The dust swirled up, the horses whinnied and neighed, the foot soldiers yelled out their warlike cries. Achilles was at the head of the Achaeans, eager to avenge the death of Patroclus. Hector had opted to stay among his men. The moment when the two armies clashed was dreadful. The air was filled with the sound of metal against metal, man against man, life against life.

Achilles looked for Hector but couldn't see him. Other Trojans attacked him, and it cost them their lives. Only Aeneas escaped, although he was wounded. Hector was still in the background when he saw Achilles slay his youngest brother, Polydorus, the boy old King Priam loved the best; he had forbidden his son from taking part in the war. However, Polydorus longed for the glory of bringing down the greatest warrior of them all. Achilles struck him with his spear; it penetrated his navel and the point came out through his back. Polydorus bent double in terrible pain, clutching his guts in his hands.

Hector could no longer hold back but rushed forward, holding his spear like a torch. Achilles rejoiced.

At last! The man who has caused me more pain than anyone else! Now we can no longer avoid each other, he said to himself.

It was Hector who hurled his spear first. Fleet-footed Achilles had no problem avoiding it. He thought his own weapon found its mark, although he couldn't see too well because of the thick dust swirling all around them. He stepped forward, slashing with his sword. There was no one there. Three times he swung his sword, each time in vain. He realized that Hector had disappeared.

A sudden gust of wind picked up even more dust, and the combatants could see virtually nothing. When it settled they ran at one another with fresh rage.

Achilles flailed wildly around him. Dryops was stabbed in the neck and fell at his feet like an empty sack. Achilles left him there and went for Demuchus, pinning him down with his spear before finishing him off with his sword. He dragged the two unfortunate brothers, Laogonus and Dardanus, from their chariot and slew them. The next man, Tros, dropped to his knees in front of Achilles and begged for mercy, but not a trace was left in Achilles's heart. Tros clasped his legs and pleaded with him, weeping, but Achilles drove his sword into the other man's liver. Black blood spurted out, along with his life. He killed Mulius by thrusting his spear into one ear and out through the other. He struck Echlecus over the head with his sword so that the blood gushed out, then he chopped off Deucalion's head. Rhigmus died when the spear pierced his stomach, and his charioteer when it penetrated his back as he tried to flee.

Raging like a fire in a dry forest Achilles drove his horses from place to place with death at his side. His chariot was black with blood, his hands were covered in blood, but he was not satisfied. He kept on going, chasing down the enemy with a fury greater than that of the goddesses of vengeance, the Erinyes.

The Myrmidons, who were well rested, succeeded in driving a wedge through the Trojans. Some—most, in fact—fled to the city and sought refuge behind its walls. A smaller group was forced down to the river and had no choice but to throw themselves into the fast-flowing waters. It wasn't easy to swim in their armor; they sank and struggled desperately. Achilles and his riders followed them into the torrent and slew them one after the other. The river turned red with blood. Even the horses reared up in protest, but the Achaeans continued in spite of the heartfelt pleas for mercy, in spite of the fact that the Trojans were unable to defend themselves, in spite of the fact that this was no longer a battle but a slaughter.

Achilles outdid himself in cruelty. When he tired of killing he leaned against a tree on the riverbank, lowered his spear, and blessed himself.

"How handsome and magnificent I am at this moment!" he said aloud as he tried to forget, just for a moment, that he too was mortal, that his strong body would one day fall to a spear or a sword. It could be today, in a month, in a year. The thought of death did not soften his heart. Quite the reverse, in fact. If he was going to die he wanted to take as many as possible with him, particularly the sons of Priam.

After a short rest he entered the swirling waters once more and picked out twelve young men. Not one or two, but twelve. They were to be spared until later. He bound their hands with leather straps and told his men to take them down to the hollow ships. They were youths, little more than boys; they should never have been part of the war. However, as the saying goes, he whose fate it is to die will never drown. Those twelve boys did not drown in the cold waters of the Scamander, because another fate awaited them. They had a good idea of what was going to happen. Some wept openly, while others lamented loudly. Their cries reached all the way across the plain to Troy, where their mothers were keeping the bean soup hot until their sons came home from battle.

Achilles still hadn't had enough. One of Priam's illegitimate sons fell to his knees before him, begging for his life. To no avail. Eventually there was no one left worth killing. A handful were still alive, men who had lost an arm or a leg, who had deep wounds to the chest or stomach; their cries were heartrending as they pleaded for someone to save them from drowning. The Achaeans, with Achilles at their head, turned their backs on the dying and set off after the stream of Trojans seeking sanctuary in the city. Some were seriously wounded, others so exhausted that their comrades had to carry them all the way from the battlefield to the Gate of the Shadows, which had been kept open on the orders of King Priam. He was standing on top of the wall and could see what was happening. He had seen his beloved son Polydorus fall down dead, and his heart was close to breaking. He cursed old age, which prevented him from being out there with his sons and the other warriors. It was essential that as many as possible should return to the city, so the magnificent gate stayed open, and the people in the square received the fleeing soldiers. Women searched for their men, children for their fathers, mothers for their sons.

Helen searched for Paris, but there was no sign of him.

Andromache searched for Hector and spotted him in the crowd.

When the Gate of the Shadows had been closed and secured with heavy wooden bars, there was only one man who remained outside.

Hector.

He stood alone. Anyone planning to conquer his city and rob the people of their freedom would have to kill him first. In the distance he could see Achilles and the Myrmidons with their brown shields approaching.

Miss wiped her forehead with a white handkerchief, which she then tucked into her sleeve with an almost unconscious gesture. I loved every little thing she did. The way her lips moved when she spoke, the way she pushed her hair to one side, the way she stretched, the way she walked, and the way she stood still.

"Come along—we're going to the square," she said, and that's what we did. Almost the entire village had gathered there.

There was a rumor that the partisan the Germans were looking for was injured. The dogs had found bloodstains on the ground, but he was gone.

"Is it definitely a man?" Miss asked.

There was nothing definite about it. More and more young women were getting involved in the resistance movement.

The period of grace granted to the village by the German captain was due to run out at sunset. All the men from the village were in the square—not that there were many of them, and most were really old. The captain wanted a bigger choice, so he lowered the age limit: Anyone from the age of sixteen now counted as a man.

The previous day Miss had called upon me to be a man when she told me to look after Dimitra. Now the German captain did the same. I hadn't turned sixteen, but I had certainly turned fifteen. Berlin was being defended by boys even younger than me, the captain said, and the mayor translated his comment.

My mother tore at her hair. She wanted to go to the mayor, to the captain himself, to the village priest. I asked her not to. There was no point. She swallowed her heart, as she put it, and stayed at home.

Farmers do not sit and admire the sunset. Right now everyone was hoping that the sun would never go down, but of course it did, with pomp and circumstance. An explosion of colors over the mountains, then a breeze heavy with an assortment of scents reached us at the last minute before the sun disappeared.

There were twelve of us in total, lined up in the church square, as we called the sheltered cobbled area in front of the church. Several men had been spared because they were very old, or because they served the Germans in one way or another. The butcher, for example, and others with useful professions. In other words, you could say that the chosen twelve wouldn't cost the Germans anything.

A masked man walked to and fro in front of us, staring at us from behind the mask, weighing up the situation with himself or with his God, who knows. He pointed to my neighbor on the left who had a harelip; he was an unfortunate soul without any property. The masked man stopped in front of me and looked at me for a long time, but decided to move on. Instead he picked out two others on the end of the line on my right. Both did odd jobs to make a living and had no land of their own. The Germans took these three with them and drove off.

Until that point you could have heard a pin drop. There was absolute silence in the square. As soon as the jeep disappeared the assembled villagers let out a cry of despair that made the birds rise from the trees where they had settled for the night.

My mother came running and took me in her arms. I hadn't been afraid, simply because I felt totally detached. I had observed what was going on as if it were a film that didn't really concern me. However, fear had set its mark upon my body; I had wet myself. My mother noticed; she took off her apron and tied it around my waist.

"Best if we dress our boys as girls," she said.

"Achilles's mother dressed him as a girl, but it didn't help," I replied.

The families of the three men who had been taken away grieved all night. The neighbors brought food for them and the children, while Miss looked after the very young ones, and Dimitra helped her.

Well over fifty years have passed since that night. I have forgotten the shame I felt at the urine stains on my pants in front of the whole village. However, I have never forgotten the weeping of those women. I can still hear it. I will hear it for as long as I live.

Sixteen

THE FOLLOWING DAY wasn't like any other day in the village. People were up early. They sat outside the cafés waiting for the mayor. He was the only one who might know what had happened to the three men. But he didn't know either.

"We'll just have to pretend that it's an ordinary day," Miss said. So we went to school and she resumed her story.

The Trojans were afraid. They stood side by side behind the walls like fawns when a storm threatens. There was no storm; instead a hot wind blew, making them sweat even more. They tried to slake their thirst. The Achaeans were getting closer, with Achilles in his chariot at their head. He shone like the constellation Orion in the fall, when it can be seen by all the people on earth.

Only Hector remained outside the Gate of the Shadows, awaiting his fate. His father, Priam, pleaded with him.

"My son, do not stand there alone. The man racing toward you will be the death of you. He is stronger. I wish with all my heart that he was dead, that dogs and vultures were ripping his body to shreds. He has slain so many of my sons. Their mother, blessed Laothoe, is beside me weeping. The people of Troy fear your death more than anything. Only you can save them—but not out there, all alone. You can lead them safely from inside these walls. I beg of you, Hector. My life is running out and my misery only increases. Several of my sons are dead, my daughters have been abducted and enslaved, my house has become a house of mourning, my grandchildren lie slain upon the ground, my daughters-in-law are caressed by the murderous hands of the Achaeans. I will also be torn apart by my own dogs, which I reared to guard my home, when a sharp spear causes my limbs to fail me. They will drink my blood, and their savage instincts will be reawakened. When a young man lies dead, his beauty remains even in death. But is there a more disgusting sight than an old man like me, his corpse defiled by dogs eating his manhood?"

Though Priam tore at his white hair, his pleas were in vain. Hector wasn't listening. Then his mother, Hecuba, stepped forward. She was Priam's first wife, and Hector was not only her firstborn but also the son she had wanted— strong, fleet-footed, magnificent. So she pushed aside the folds of her robe and exposed her left breast as she addressed him in her deep voice.

"My beloved son, with this breast I fed you and comforted you when you were hungry or upset. Have mercy on your father and me. Defend yourself and the city from behind these walls. Do not face your dreadful foe alone and outside the walls. If you fall out there, then neither I, your mother, nor Andromache, your wife, will be able to grieve at your bier; your body will be torn to pieces by the Achaeans' dogs over by their black ships."

Hector fixed his gaze on a point in the distance in order to resist his mother's prayers. The situation became even more difficult when Andromache appeared on top of the wall with their son in her arms. The little boy waved to his father, whose resolve faltered for a moment. Perhaps he should enter the city—but he had refused to do so before, because he had trusted in his own strength. Now there was a risk of dragging the whole of Troy to destruction along with him. It might be better to seek refuge behind the walls—but then he would no longer be the man he was. His fate was to remain here and either defeat Achilles or fall with his honor intact.

Then he had an idea.

He placed his shield and helmet on the ground, then propped his spear up against the wall. He had decided to meet Achilles unarmed in order to seek reconciliation. Helen would be returned, along with everything she had brought with her. All the treasures of the wealthy city would be divided equally between Achaeans and Trojans. It was an appealing picture, but Hector knew that Achilles was not a man who could forgive, that he would slay him like a defenseless woman. It would be impossible to conduct a conversation with a man who was so enraged. The only option was the worst scenario of all: Hector must face his opponent in deadly single combat, and hope that the gods would be with him.

These were his thoughts as Achilles came closer and closer. Hector was not a coward, but he saw death approaching. His heart burst and he took to his heels. All the city gates were closed, so he ran around below the walls hoping to find a place where he could sneak inside.

Achilles pursued him like a hawk. They passed the watchtower and the old fig tree; they ran toward the two springs that fed the river. One gave ice-cold water even in summer, the other flowed with warm water even in winter. That was where the women used to do their laundry in fine troughs with gleaming stones in the bottom—in peacetime, of course. It was many years since any woman had ventured down to the spring.

One hero was chasing another. The people up on the walls had never seen anything like it. They shouted encouragement to Hector and cursed Achilles, even though the two runners could hear nothing but their own breathing and the blood pounding in their ears.

Andromache couldn't bear it. Her little son asked, "Why is Daddy running?" She had no answer, but Helen cheerfully told him, "They're just having a race to see who's fastest."

Death might not be the fastest, but he catches up with all of us. Andromache took her child and went home. She wanted to spare both the boy and herself from seeing the outcome of that race, which would end with one of the competitors, her husband or his opponent, lying dead at the foot of the walls.

Everyone else stayed where they were, leaning over to get a better view of the two men speeding along like thoroughbred horses. It reminded them of a dream. Hector couldn't get away, Achilles couldn't catch him.

Three times they went around the city walls, and the distance between them remained the same. The audience grew impatient, something had to happen, there had to be a resolution. They shouted to Hector to stop and fight.

"Almighty Zeus is on your side, Hector! He has not forgotten all those occasions when you sacrificed fat bulls to him! If the time has come to fulfill your fate, then do it!"

Some of them even started placing bets. The deadly single combat between the two heroes was turning into something of a circus act, and everyone wanted to see how it ended. Even Hector's brother—one of the few who was still alive—called to him to stop and fight man to man, spear to spear, sword to sword.

Meanwhile people had started emerging from the Achaeans' tents and ships: wounded warriors, servants, Trojan prisoners of war, slave girls, each one with his or her own hopes. The Achaeans dreamed that they would soon be able to board their ships, hoist the sails, and set off for home. The Trojans hoped to regain their lives if Hector was victorious. Briseis, who had also joined the others, was not in such a fortunate position. She both loathed and worshipped Achilles. Her head told her that she ought to wish him dead, but her heart had a different message.

There was no doubt that the chase was taking its toll on Hector's strength more than on his opponent's. Fear weakened him, while rage made Achilles even stronger. Hector could no longer avoid his fate, and so he stopped.

Silence fell, and Hector spoke into that silence.

"I will no longer flee, Achilles. I stand here ready to face you, ready to kill or be killed. But first I want to make a promise to you. If the gods grant me victory, I will not defile your body. I will take your armor, but I will return your body to your countrymen. Promise me that you will do the same."

Achilles's heroic barbarity did not allow him to show any humanity, and he simply sneered at Hector.

"I have never heard of a pact between a lion and a man, or between a wolf and a lamb. I feel nothing but anger toward you because of all the friends and comrades of mine that you have slain. Your time has come."

He had barely finished speaking when he hurled his spear, but Hector made himself so small that it flew over him. Was this a sign from the gods? Did they want to give him the glory of bringing down the Achaeans' greatest warrior?

"You missed, Achilles, and I am still here! I am not going to run away—you will not see my back!"

Hector threw his own spear with renewed confidence. It struck the center of Achilles's shield but did not penetrate it, which dismayed Hector.

I have no intention of dying without honor and without a fight, he said to himself. He seized his heavy sword and rocked back and forth on his toes for a moment, gathering his strength like an eagle that hovers in the sky before swooping on a grazing lamb.

Achilles was not unprepared. He had already chosen his target: the point where the throat and collarbone meet. There and only there. Everything else was protected by armor.

The two men were a magnificent sight—Hector with his dark curls and those passionate, coal-black eyes; Achilles with his long fair hair and feline yellow eyes. Tall, broad-shouldered, and narrow-hipped. If the supreme god had any sense he would let them both live. That didn't happen.

This time Achilles did not miss. His spear penetrated Hector's neck. He fell to the ground but was still able to speak.

"I beg you, do not throw my body to the dogs. My father and mother will reward you generously with gold, silver, and bronze if you will only allow them to take me home so that the Trojans and their wives may burn me on a funeral pyre, as is our custom."

This enraged Achilles still more.

"Do not plead with me, you cur! I would like to hack you to pieces and eat your raw flesh in revenge for the pain you caused me when you slew my dearest friend. No treasures in the world can save you now. If your father offered me your weight in gold, your mother would still not be permitted to lay you on a bier and sing her laments over you. You do not belong to them anymore. You belong to the dogs and the carrion birds."

Hector summoned the last of his strength. He shook his head and his helmet gleamed as in days gone by.

"Your heart is harder than your spear; I shouldn't ask for your mercy. But your day will also come. However brave you might be, you are not immortal."

This was the last thing Hector said, and death closed his eyes with cold fingers.

Achilles had to have the final word.

"I will welcome my death when it comes."

He pulled out his spear and put it to one side, dripping with blood, then stripped the body of its armor. A number of the Achaeans crowded around and couldn't help admiring Hector's beauty even in death, although that didn't stop them from attacking the naked corpse with stabs and blows, with kicks, spitting, curses, and spiteful abuse.

"He doesn't have as much to say for himself now as when he was trying to set our ships on fire!"

Achilles still wasn't satisfied. His ferocious heart cried out for more revenge and still more revenge, so that no one

would ever forget it, so that even the gods would be astonished. He made holes in the dead man's feet and through
these holes he threaded strong leather straps, which he then
tied to his chariot. The others looked on, trying to work out
what he had in mind. It soon became clear.

Achilles drove off, dragging the corpse along the ground,
and Hector's once handsome face was covered in dust. The
black curls trailed in the dirt, his nose was broken, the half-
open mouth collected sand and dust and the waste from the
horses.

Hecuba, Hector's mother, screamed and tried to throw
herself from the high wall. Priam, his father, wept loudly. He
wanted to go out and plead with Achilles, but his people
stopped him. "He is too cruel and too angry," they said, but
Priam was still determined to try.

"He might respect my age. His father is as old as me. I
have already suffered enough. Several of my sons are dead,
and now I have lost the one who was most precious to me.
When you lose those you love, the only solace comes from
mourning them with dignity, from holding them in your arms,
wailing and lamenting until you have had your fill."

Hecuba would never have her fill. Surrounded by her
daughters-in-law and other women, she spoke to her son.

"How can I live with this pain? You were my pride and
joy, the pride and defender of the whole city. You were
my glory and the glory of Troy. How am I going to live
without you?"

The only person who didn't know about Hector's death was Andromache. She hadn't dared to stay by the wall but had gone home, sat down at her loom, and pretended that everything was normal. She told the slave girls with the pretty braided hair to heat the water ready for Hector's bath when he returned home from the conflict. From time to time she glanced at her son, who was sleeping close by in the arms of his wet nurse. Suddenly, for no apparent reason, she was gripped by fear; her body shook and she dropped her shuttle. She could hear groans and sorrowful voices in the distance. She leaped to her feet and took two slave girls with her. What misfortune had befallen the city?

She ran to the wall, her heart pounding as if it were trying to break out of her breast. Someone tried to stop her from seeing what she had already seen. Her husband was being dragged along behind Achilles's chariot, which was speeding toward the Achaeans' ships. A darkness darker than the night shrouded her eyes and she collapsed on the stony ground. Her golden headdress slipped off, taking with it the veil that held her long, wavy hair in place.

It was Helen who took care of her and revived her.

"My husband, my Hector!" Andromache wailed. "I have lost everything!"

The tears poured down her face and her voice failed her. It would have been better if she had never been born, better if she had never given birth to a son, who would now grow up without his father. Helen rocked her in her arms, and Andromache remembered when Hector had come to her father with rich gifts and asked for her hand in marriage, before Achilles had destroyed her city. She remembered their first night together, and fresh tears flowed. The body she loved would be consumed by dogs and vultures. She would not have the chance to kiss him before his final departure. All that was left of him were his clothes, woven by the women of Troy. She would burn those clothes on a great pyre.

"What is our son going to do without you, my husband? Who will protect him from dangerous games, who will teach him to tame a horse and throw a spear? Who will make him a man? Your quest for honor and glory in war, that source of tears, has led to your death. You left your son and me when we had only just tasted happiness."

With these words Andromache wept once more.

Miss sat down.

"That will do for today," she said, fixing her gaze on me. It had become a habit. Each time she stopped for the day, she turned to me—but this time she really was looking hard at me.

Why? Was she thinking about the previous evening, when I stood before the masked man in the square? Was she thinking that I would soon be there again?

Did she have any idea how I felt about her? Do we smell different when we're in love? Maybe. Dimitra had definitely seen through me, and gave me a sympathetic smile.

We walked home together as usual.

"What a terrible person Achilles was! He's like the Germans. How on earth can they sacrifice innocent people just for the sake of revenge?"

I agreed with her. How indeed?

When we reached the square we found the answer. They just do. They do it because they can. The three men who had been picked out yesterday were hanging from the ancient chestnut tree.

"They look so helpless," Dimitra said, her voice almost inaudible. Being hanged is a very cruel way to die. You are robbed of contact with the earth. You die exiled from your element, in the emptiness of the air.

I put my arm around her shoulders and led her away. Miss had made me responsible for Dimitra. The families of the dead were no longer weeping.

"Life goes on," I said. I knew it was stupid, but I couldn't come up with anything better. In a couple of hours, three new victims would be selected. In a couple of hours I would be standing in line with the others, and the masked man would point at three of us.

Was I going to die tonight?

I thought about all the innocent young men whom Achilles had murdered, showing no mercy. More than three thousand years had passed since then, and death had not become any less cruel.

I had definitely decided that I wasn't going to wet myself again. It was the least I could do.

I climbed up into the mulberry tree, as high as it was possible to get. That was what we used to do as little boys—a test of manhood. From there I was able to follow the transit of the sun. The shadows slowly grew longer, the mountains in the distance grew darker. The fragrance of the almond blossoms mingled with more robust cooking smells from the houses all around: oregano and basil, rancid fat, bean soup. It seemed to me that even the sunlight had a scent of its own.

Then the church bell signaled that it was evening, and time to go to the square. My mother was looking for me, but I couldn't bear to say goodbye to her yet again.

The men from the village were outside the church, and I joined the end of the line. The German captain and the masked man were already there.

As we waited, more dead than alive, a military vehicle came speeding into the square. They had caught the partisan. Miss had been right: It didn't necessarily have to be a man. It could be a woman, and it was a woman. We'd never seen her before, but then again we wouldn't have recognized her anyway.

They threw her on the ground like a sack of wheat. Her body was covered in blood, but she was alive. She was whimpering very quietly. The captain and his colleague in the car held a brief discussion. No one heard what was said, but everyone saw what happened next. The captain shot the young woman, right in the middle of her forehead. Her brains spattered all around. Then he spoke to the mayor, who translated his decision.

Yes, they had caught the person they were looking for, but after sunset. Therefore three of us would be executed, as he had decreed.

And that's what happened. Three new victims were selected, I wasn't one of them. The Germans took them and drove away. They left the young woman on the cobbles outside the church.

"We need to find out who she is," the mayor said.

At that moment Miss stepped forward. The woman was her colleague and friend from the nearby mountain village. The Germans had carried out a raid and set fire to it. The wind carried the thick smoke and the smell of burning flesh all the way over to us.

"I'll take care of her. Her name is Iphigenia," Miss said.

"Iphigenia...what?" asked the mayor.

Miss shook her head. "It doesn't matter."

Then she turned to me.

"Will you help me?" she asked.

Seventeen

Miss wiped her eyes, and so did the rest of us, especially Dimitra. It had been a long night. The whole village had kept vigil. We took care of the young woman's body, washing away the blood and semen. They had forced themselves on her, using every orifice.

Miss fetched her prettiest dress and put it on her friend. The grandmother of one of the three men who had been executed the previous day sang a lament in her shaky voice.

> *My child, how shall I bear*
> *so much pain?*
> *If I scatter it over hill and dale*
> *the birds will peck at it.*
> *If I cast it into the sea*
> *the fish will nibble at it.*
> *If I lay it at the crossroads*
> *the wanderers will trample upon it.*

I would rather hold it in my heart.
Then I can lie down and rest for a while
when it hurts too much.

Everyone who was there struggled to hold back the tears. Dimitra rested her head on my shoulder. She was my responsibility. Miss had said so.

The burial was very discreet. It took place early in the morning, just as the sun broke through the mist. We were afraid of arousing the Germans' anger, but we couldn't do anything at night. God must know who had died.

However, two Germans did show up. They didn't come close, they didn't make it obvious, it was almost as if they just happened to be near the churchyard.

It was the two pilots, Wolfgang and Erich. Miss lowered her head to hide a little smile, a newborn baby of a smile, you could say.

But I saw it. And I knew. They were in love, all three of them. One woman and two men. How was that going to end?

Eighteen

THE NEXT DAY was the first of May. Dimitra and I cut across the square on our way to school. Posters had been put up outside the three cafés and the mayor's office, and on the big chestnut tree. It was from the German area commandant. Due to the Greek resistance fighters' "cowardly" murder of a high-ranking German officer, two hundred political prisoners in various jails had been executed, with "outstanding bravery" as Dimitra read scornfully.

I immediately thought about my father. Was he still alive?

I squeezed my eyes tight shut, as if I didn't want to see what I saw. Could I keep it from my mother?

We had almost arrived at school. Miss was pale, with dark circles beneath her eyes.

"There's nothing we can do apart from our job," she said, and continued her story in a slightly unsteady voice.

Andromache mourned her husband, surrounded by the women of Troy, and Achilles prepared to lead the lament for Patroclus. The Achaeans had returned to their ships and dispersed. But the Myrmidons gathered around their leader, and he spoke to them.

"My loyal friends and comrades, let us not step down from our chariots and unharness our horses with their long manes. Instead let us honor Patroclus as befits a man who struck fear into the hearts of our enemy. Then we will eat together and talk about him, about his beauty and strength, his steadfast friendship and warm heart, until our grief eases."

Three times they drove their horses around Patroclus's bier, weeping and watering the sand with the tears pouring down their faces, until Achilles descended from his chariot and positioned himself in front of the dead man.

"I have kept the promise I made to you, my beloved friend. Hector lies dead, and soon I will feed him to the dogs."

He flung Hector's body before the bier and kicked it. After that he was calm enough to offer the men an excellent meal. Huge quantities of oxen and calves, sheep and lambs, full-grown goats and kids, fat hogs and suckling pigs were slaughtered, flayed, and grilled over open fires.

Achilles ate nothing and drank nothing.

Meanwhile a message arrived from Agamemnon, inviting Achilles to his tent along with all the other leaders and kings.

Victory was close. Hector, the incorruptible defender of Troy, was as dead as he could be.

Agamemnon's servants had heated water so that Achilles could wash off the blood and dust. He refused.

"I do not have the right to enjoy anything until I have sent my friend on his way, raised a monument to his memory, and cut my hair. However long I live, I will never experience such pain again. But if you want to please me, Agamemnon, order your servants to gather everything that is needed for a magnificent pyre—both young and mature oaks that will burn easily and smell good. My friend must reach the King of the Underworld wreathed in burning flames, which can dispel the darkness of death for a little while."

Agamemnon promised to take care of the matter, and Achilles returned to his men, who had gone to their tents to rest. He couldn't sleep. He was very tired, but slumber would not come, and in the end he went and sat on the shore. A cooling breeze blew in from the east, carrying with it the wailing and weeping of the Trojans.

It was Patroclus's fate to be killed by Hector. It was Hector's fate to be killed by Achilles. *Who or what will be my fate?* he asked himself. He would have liked to have Briseis by his side right now. She could always lull him to sleep with her caresses. The very thought of her made him relax, and he fell into an uneasy doze, suffused with bad dreams and disturbing images. The pursuit of Hector below the walls of Troy, in full view of everyone, had made him feel more like an executioner than a hero. But most of all he was tormented by the appearance of Patroclus in his dream, upbraiding him bitterly.

"How can you sleep, Achilles? You were my loyal friend in life, but not in death. I am left wandering outside the gates of Hades; the shades of dead heroes and kings will not let me enter, because you have not burned my body. Give me your hand for one last time. You also have a fate that awaits you, but promise me that you will preserve my ashes in the same golden urn that is meant for you. Do not let me lie far from you!"

Thus spoke Patroclus in the dream. Achilles reached up to embrace his friend, but there was nothing to embrace. This emptiness was so palpable that it woke him, just as silence can sometimes be louder than howling wolves.

The day dawned behind Mount Ida, shimmering like a bride on the way to her wedding. Agamemnon kept his promise. His men were already busy felling young and mature oaks, then chopping them into logs that would burn easily before piling them up in the place Achilles had chosen.

Then Achilles ordered the Myrmidons to put on their armor and harness the horses to the chariots. They led the parade, followed by thousands of foot soldiers, like a brown cloud. The bier was carried by four great warriors, and the body was covered in hair. All of the Achaeans, who were known for wearing their hair long, had cut their locks and thrown them on the corpse.

Achilles was supporting his friend's head so that he could personally hand him over to death. When they reached the pyre he cut off a lock of his own thick golden hair and placed it in Patroclus's stiff hands.

Many wept, and they would weep until the sun went down on their grief, but Achilles asked Agamemnon to send the troops back to their ships to have their evening meal.

Only Patroclus's closest friends stayed behind. With great sadness they lifted his body onto the pyre, which was almost twelve feet wide and twelve feet high. They then slaughtered a large number of sheep and oxen. Achilles smeared the corpse with fat from the animals and piled their flayed bodies around Patroclus. He added urns filled with oil and honey, followed by four horses. But that wasn't enough. He cut the throats of two of his nine dogs, which he was in the habit of feeding at his table.

But the worst, the most shameful task remained. A short distance from the pyre were the twelve young Trojans Achilles had taken from the river. They had been watching the proceedings with growing terror. When they were little they had no doubt dreamed of becoming heroes, admired and loved by beautiful women, being the subject of songs and exciting tales. Now they were sitting on the soft sand with their hands and feet bound, close to one another yet not together. Each was thinking about his own family or his sweetheart. Each was thinking about his own death. They would have no grave, their living bodies would turn to ashes. That was what they were thinking, and they wept quietly. They knew that nothing and no one could help them.

Not many people are adept in the art of cutting the throat of a goat or a sheep. Even fewer can slit the throat of a human being with one stroke, but Achilles could, and he was the cruelest of them all. One by one the young Trojans were brought to him as he stood there, legs wide apart, his sharp sword in his hand. He wanted to look them in the eye. He wanted them to look him in the eye. He wanted to be the last thing they saw.

And he was.

Their blood spurted over him, but he continued, possessed by an unholy rage. Even some of the older leaders thought he had gone too far, but they said nothing.

Finally he picked up two burning torches, one in each hand, and shouted as loudly as he could so that his dead friend would be able to hear him: "Hail to you, Patroclus; may you enter the Kingdom of the Dead. I have fulfilled all the promises I made to you. Twelve young sons of noble Trojan houses will keep you company in the flames. But not your murderer. The dogs will feed on Hector."

It was the strangest thing: The fire refused to catch, and the dogs wouldn't touch Hector's corpse.

The gods must have loved him very much, Achilles thought, feeling something that was close to sympathy for the man he had defiled so grossly.

The lull didn't last for long. Suddenly a strong wind blew up; this was quite common along the coast of Troy. It had gained speed as it passed through the narrow sound farther up and came in fierce gusts. Sometimes they lasted for only a few minutes, sometimes days and nights on end. This time the gale went on for hours, causing the fire to burn with great ferocity. Achilles watched over the blaze all night, wetting the ground with wine to prevent it from spreading. From time to time he sat down and wept loudly.

When the morning star rose in the sky, the pyre had collapsed and the fire was almost extinguished. The wind abated, but out at sea the waves were still high. Achilles was exhausted after all the slaughtering and his long vigil, and he lay down for a while. Slumber came to him, padding softly like a cat, and he was asleep before he even knew it.

———————

Miss decided to stop there for the day.

"We will let Achilles rest for a while. Tomorrow is another day," she said. She was tired. So were we.

Dimitra and I left together, but instead of going straight home we went via the square. The German captain was sitting with the mayor, while Wolfgang and Erich were at another table.

They were losing the war, and it showed. Their uniforms hadn't been pressed and there were holes in the soles of their unpolished boots.

In some ways we felt sorry for them.

"They're not much older than us," Dimitra said.

At that moment Miss appeared, and the two young men both got to their feet. She smiled and joined them.

She suddenly looked happy.

But as she'd said, tomorrow was another day, and no one knew how that day would go.

Dimitra stared at her as if she were under a spell.

"I wish I was as brave as her," she said.

We didn't stay long in the square. When we were about to go our separate ways under the mulberry tree, Dimitra said no one was home at her house. Her mother was visiting her own mother in the next village, and her father was in the taverna.

I heard what she said and I knew what she meant. Did I dare to go with her? I was in love with someone else. I was in love with Miss, who was sitting outside a café with two German pilots. She wasn't in love with me, but that was her problem. Not mine.

So I went home. My mother was waiting for me; she had seen the poster about the two hundred prisoners who had been executed, but something told her that her husband wasn't one of them.

Who was she trying to convince? Me or herself?

"I'm sure you're right, Mom. Dad's alive. Just like you and me."

She'd had me when she was eighteen years old. She was thirty-three now, and I almost felt as if we were the same age.

"Mom, I'm in love," I said.

She leaped to her feet.

"With Dimitra?" she said, her voice full of warmth.

When I saw her happiness, I didn't want to cloud it. I didn't say "yes" and I didn't say "no."

Instead I just said, teasingly, "Who knows?"

Nineteen

MY GRANDMOTHER HAD MADE a decision. She was going to set off and find out where my father was being held, if he was still alive. She couldn't allow her daughter to live in a state of uncertainty. My grandfather tried to persuade her to stay home.

"It's too dangerous out there, my Maria," he said.

He was right. In the final days of the war, Greece was a slaughterhouse. The Germans executed people, their Greek collaborators executed people, the resistance movement executed people. However, my grandmother said she could no longer watch her daughter wasting away in sorrow.

She was small and skinny, my grandmother, always in a black dress. Toothless, with breathing difficulties and a cough. But off she went. Her provisions consisted of an onion, a few olives, and a piece of bread. My mother and I said goodbye to her early in the morning.

"Grandma is a saint," Mom said. For some reason I'd counted the olives she'd taken with her. Seven small wrinkled olives. Back then I had no idea that I would never forget it. That as a grown man many years later, I would always have seven olives with my breakfast. No more, no less. But on that particular day I was in a rush to get to school to hear the next part of Miss's story.

Achilles hadn't finished mourning. In spite of all the animals he'd slaughtered, in spite of the twelve young Trojans he'd sacrificed. Their mothers' wailing and lamenting could be heard across the plain and caused many hard-bitten warriors to pause for a moment and consider the insanity of war and Achilles's immeasurable grief. There was one last thing that could be done: funeral games in memory of the deceased.

There were plenty of prizes, everything from gold to women with multicolored girdles. There were competitions in boxing, wrestling, running, spear throwing, and chariot racing. The outcome was the same as it always was when the Achaeans competed among themselves: cheating and disputes, false accusations, dirty tricks, insults, and corrupt officials.

Odysseus managed to bring down mighty Ajax in a wrestling bout by kicking him on the legs—which was forbidden—and came second in running even though he was the oldest. He had taken a short cut. Only in boxing was the victory crystal clear, because the winner simply killed his opponent with a series of repeated blows to the head.

Agamemnon won the spear throwing without even competing, because everyone knew he was the best, but to his credit he gave the prize to his herald.

At least the games provided good entertainment for the troops and a welcome break from the battle.

Evening came, and the men returned to their ships and tents to eat and sleep.

Achilles didn't want to eat, and he couldn't sleep. Briseis was waiting in his tent, but he lay on the shore tossing and turning, weeping and howling, then got up and wandered around as if he were trying to get away from himself. He thought about all the occasions when he and Patroclus had fought side by side, running through enemy lines or sailing on stormy seas.

That was how he spent the night, and when dawn came he tied Hector's body to his chariot and drove three times around Patroclus's funeral mound. This made him feel a little better, and he went back to his tent to rest. He stank of blood, sweat, and horse.

Briseis could no longer keep quiet.

"I don't recognize you. For days now you have wept and killed, killed and wept. You have defiled Hector, who did what you should have done: defended his people and his city. He was your equal, but the gods were on your side and you defeated him. You ought to let his wife and son, his mother and father, his friends and the people of Troy see him again, say their goodbyes, mourn him, and burn him on a pyre as befits a man who gave his life for them. It is a good thing to be gracious in the hour of defeat, but it is even better to be gracious in the hour of victory. I have heated the water. Go and wash yourself, and come back to me as the man I know. You have not lain with me since my return. Vengeance is more attractive to you than I am. Last night when I slept for a little while, Zeus came to me in a dream and spoke very clearly: 'Tell Achilles that it is not human to grieve so much. Life comes and life goes. His too. Tell him to return Hector's body to his family and his people rather than leaving his corpse rotting by the ships. Otherwise he will arouse my anger, and neither he nor anyone else, mortal or immortal, wants to do that.'"

Achilles listened to her, not because he wanted to but because he couldn't help it. Her clear voice washed away the noise of battle, the animalistic affirmation of all the killing. He wanted to be a man again, the man she recognized.

"I will do as you wish," he said, stepping into the warm water. Briseis washed him from top to toe as his mother used to do when he was a child.

In the arms of a woman we all become little children, he thought before falling into a deep sleep.

Briseis took this as a sign and didn't waste time hesitating. She dressed in a soft, shimmering black robe that reached down to her well-turned ankles. A servant saddled up the horse Achilles had given her, a young stallion from Argos, city of the swift horses. She set off for Troy with the sun at her back. As she approached the Gate of the Shadows she could hear the sound of weeping and wailing from Priam's palace. The guards led her to him.

He was sitting in the great hall with the members of his family who had been spared by the war so far: his younger sons and daughters, his daughters-in-law, and his grandchildren. Paris was the only one of his grown-up sons who was still alive, but he was with the army.

Helen wasn't there either; she was alone in her room. How could she bring herself to be with the others? How could she possibly console Andromache? Did she even have the right to try? The guilt and shame grew in her heart like a tumor. So many people had died because of the love she and Paris shared. She couldn't eat, drink, sleep, or wake up properly. Even Paris's caresses disgusted her. His hands felt as repulsive as snakes on her body. When she was still living in Sparta, she had once seen the skin of a snake. It was exactly like the reptile itself, but the snake was gone. That was how she felt now, as if she were leaving her body and her senses.

The old king's face, smeared with earth, ash, and tears, had stiffened in a mask of grief and horror. The women around him mourned their husbands, the children their fathers.

"Are you bringing more bad news, my daughter?" Priam said to Briseis. He had known her ever since she was a little girl; her father had been a good friend of his. She was a king's daughter who had become a captive and a slave.

"My king, I bring a message from Achilles. He has agreed to hand over Hector's body to you, and he will accept the gifts you offer him in return. But there is one condition."

"I will do anything," Priam said.

"You must go to Achilles's tent alone. You may take one elderly unarmed servant to drive your chariot, but no one else. He promises that he will not lay a hand on you; he has changed his mind and wants Hector to be honored as befits him. Take the sturdiest cart with the most ornate wheels to convey your gifts to Achilles and your son's body back to the city. You have nothing to fear. He has enough sense not to harm a defenseless old man."

Priam wanted to set off immediately, but thought he ought to discuss the matter with his wife first. She was totally against the idea.

"You have no reason whatsoever to trust that murderer," she said.

But Priam had made up his mind.

"If I can just see my most beloved son one last time, I don't care if I die in the attempt."

He wasn't only grieving; he was also angry. Suddenly it seemed to him that all his other sons, and indeed all the other Trojans, had no right to live when the best among them was gone. He sent everyone out of the great hall; it plagued him to see them, to hear their whining voices.

"You are not warriors! You are better suited to life as dancers, or sheep and goat thieves! Get out of my sight!"

They had never seen Priam so furious, and slunk off with their tails between their legs. He calmed down a little and ordered the cart to be prepared and laden with all the costly gifts he was going to take to Achilles. There was gold and silver, there were exquisite bowls and amphorae, finely woven fabrics, and a pair of beautiful horses that he himself had raised.

He was about to leave when Hecuba emerged from her room with a golden jug of sweet wine and exhorted him to offer a libation to almighty Zeus.

Priam softened. He had lost most of his sons, but they were Hecuba's sons too. In fact they were more her sons than his. She had carried them in her body, fed them at her breasts, comforted them when they hurt themselves. One thing was certain: His pain could not be greater than hers.

A serving girl brought fresh water from the spring. Priam washed his hands, poured wine onto the altar in the middle of the courtyard, then prayed with his gaze fixed on Mount Ida, which was visible in the distance and hid the rising sun.

"Glorious and almighty Zeus! Send me your eagle, your black messenger, as a sign of Achilles's goodwill. Let it appear from the right and fly over my home, so that I may face my son's killer with trust in my heart."

As he finished speaking the great bird soared across the sky from the right, to the joy of Hecuba and everyone else.

And so Priam and his servant left the city, secure in the knowledge that nothing bad was going to befall them. They rode for many hours; the mules pulling the cart were patient but not swift. The horses drawing Priam's chariot were swift but not as patient. It was time to let them drink and rest. The two men also slept for a little while, and in his dream Priam saw black dogs tearing Hector to pieces; that strong body was no more than a bloody rag. He cried out in his sleep, waking both himself and the servant, who asked what was wrong. The old king had tears in his eyes and couldn't bring himself to explain.

"We must hurry," was all he said.

It was late and very dark when they reached the Achaean camp. The surly guards refused to let them pass, but the servant persuaded them with a handful of gold coins.

Everywhere was in darkness. The army was sleeping, gathering strength for a decisive onslaught on Troy now that Hector was gone. But in one tent—the largest of them all—a light glowed.

Priam left his servant to watch over the horses and the cart laden with gifts, then he took a deep breath and walked into the tent.

Achilles was feasting with a group of comrades. They had eaten and drunk, bragged shamelessly, and shared coarse jokes. Briseis was the only woman present, and the old king didn't hesitate.

He bowed down laboriously before Achilles, embraced his knees and kissed his hands. A deathly silence fell. All those around the table were astonished at this intrusion—none more so than Achilles.

"Think about your father, Achilles, when you look at me. He is as old as I am, and just as weak. Perhaps he is also under threat from enemy tribes, and will face them alone and without help if a war should break out. His only joy comes from hearing that you are alive, and every day he hopes that you will return home.

"My sadness is boundless. I had fifty sons when the Achaeans arrived, nineteen of them with my two wives and the others with women in my city. Most have died in the war, and I have held their lifeless bodies in my arms. Hector was my only support, and he is dead. It is for his sake that I am here—to take his body home. I will give you what you want; out there is a cart piled high with costly gifts. Show mercy, Achilles! I have just done what no mortal man has done before: I kissed your hands, the same hands that slew my son."

Priam's words struck Achilles to the heart. He loved his father, and although the old man kneeling before him was a king and an enemy, above all he was a grieving father. He softened. He helped the weeping Priam to his feet and embraced him, and the two men stood there for a long time, overwhelmed by the memory of what they had lost— one his beloved son, the other his beloved friend. Grief has no homeland and no borders. Everyone in that tent had lost someone.

That was the harvest of war.

The silence seemed to last for an eternity, until Achilles spoke to Priam.

"You poor man, how can your heart bear everything you have had to endure?"

He admired the old king's courage in entering the wolf's lair with nothing to protect him apart from his white hair. Moreover, Priam's manner and posture reminded Achilles of his own father; both men had a dignity that could not be broken down by misfortune and suffering.

He would give Priam his son, but first he would obey the ancient laws of hospitality. The table was laid afresh, and Priam's servant was also invited in.

Priam did not want to eat and drink with his son's executioner, but he liked Achilles, whose manner and posture reminded him of Hector. They both had a power that quite simply always leads to an early death.

Meanwhile Briseis and some of the serving girls took care of Hector. They washed him, anointed him with oil, dressed him in a well-stitched cloak, and laid him on a bier. When Achilles came out to make sure that everything was as it should be, Iphis—Patroclus's woman—appeared.

"How can you so easily forget the promise you made to your friend? You said you would not return Hector to the Trojans! Were Priam's gifts so seductive?"

She was beside herself, partly because of what she regarded as Achilles's betrayal of Patroclus but also because she was afraid of him. How dare she speak to him in that way? Everyone knew how close love and anger were within him, how the hand that caressed could also strike, swiftly and to lethal effect.

Achilles did not strike her, but remained silent for a long time before he answered.

"You are right. I have gone back on my word. Not because of the gifts—you will receive half of them—but because the gods require us to show respect for the dead, even if they happen to be our enemies. That's what Patroclus would have wanted too. Now go and help Briseis and the others."

With those words he went back into the tent. Priam had eaten and drunk, and was weary.

"Tomorrow morning you can take your son home," Achilles said.

"I would like to leave right away, but I don't have the strength. Ever since Hector met his fate I haven't slept a wink. I have wallowed in my grief like a pig in his sty. Now you have given me food to eat and wine to drink. Give me a bed to lie in—that's all I need," Priam said.

Torches in hand, Achilles's servants went off in search of warm furs and red blankets, along with fine woolen cloaks. They made up two beds in the portico; the other Achaeans might easily get the wrong idea if it became known that Achilles was accommodating Priam inside his tent.

When everything was ready, Achilles had a question.

"Tell me, King Priam, how many days do you need for the funeral rites? I will keep a truce here, and restrain the army."

Priam was so moved that he had to swallow hard several times before he could respond.

"You know we are under siege. We have to fetch wood from the mountains, and we need safe passage to do so. We will mourn Hector for nine days. On the tenth day we will bury him and hold the funeral feast. On the eleventh we will raise his barrow. On the twelfth—if necessary—we can resume the battle."

Achilles clasped the old man's wrist and assured him that everything would be as he wished.

Priam soon fell asleep, as did Achilles in his comfortable bed, with Briseis by his side. But Briseis remained awake.

She waited until the night had deepened and the whole camp was silent. Then she crept out and woke Priam.

"The danger is not over yet. If Agamemnon finds out that you're here, no gifts in the world will be enough to get you away alive," she said.

Priam had been thinking along the same lines. He roused his servant, who harnessed the mules to the cart laden with Hector's bier, and the horses to Priam's chariot.

Briseis swiftly led them out of the camp, then equally swiftly returned to Achilles's bed.

One thing she knew for sure.

Heroes always sleep deeply.

Miss sat down, trying to conceal a yawn.

"That's enough for today. I too would like to enjoy a really deep sleep at some point," she said.

She was wearing an olive-green blouse and a long black skirt. She had stopped dressing entirely in black. I don't know how many people had noticed, but I had. Wasn't she grieving? Or had she found something that made her happy? A bead of sweat trickled slowly down her white throat.

I was seized by panic. I could hardly breathe.

What would it be like to live without seeing her?

Dimitra jabbed her elbow into my ribs.

"Thanks," I said.

"You're staring at her like a dog stares at a meaty bone," she said.

We headed home in silence.

We sat for a while in the cool shade of the mulberry tree. Dimitra took my hand.

"Don't be sad. You're not the only one who suffers from unrequited love. I'm in the same position, and I haven't died of it yet."

"What are you talking about? Can a person die of unrequited love?"

"It's the most common cause of death," she informed me.

She was making fun of me. She was making fun of herself. We were young and powerless, but Dimitra had discovered irony.

The fact that life smiles at us with tears in its eyes.

I glanced around. It was siesta time. People were sleeping. There was no sign of anyone, which didn't necessarily mean that no one could see us. But I didn't care.

I leaned forward and pressed my lips to hers, like a stamp. I didn't want to die without ever having kissed a girl. At the same time I was afraid she would get mad. She didn't. Instead she pressed her lips to mine, equally briefly, and said, "Everybody will be talking about us tonight."

Twenty

NOBODY WAS TALKING about us the next morning, because everybody was talking about the Germans, who had apparently been ordered to relocate. They were running back and forth packing guns, ammunition, and various necessities into their vehicles. The captain and the mayor were seen shaking hands—God knows why. Some of the local warlords who had positioned themselves on the side of the Germans were also getting ready to follow them.

The resistance movement had grown strong. It was rumored that a division of ELAS—the acronym for the Greek People's Liberation Army—was on its way to our area.

"Many mothers will weep," said my grandfather.

We didn't dare show any sign of rejoicing. We went to school as usual. Miss looked both happy and strained, but she continued with her story.

The rosy dawn swept across the plain like the faint blush on a young girl's cheeks. Priam and his servant were approaching Troy; they could already see the Gate of the Shadows. They stopped for a while with their heads bowed by the tall fig tree where Hector had fallen.

A number of men and slender-waisted women were already waiting by the wall. They saw the two men approaching but didn't recognize them. Only Priam's daughter Cassandra, who had been given the blessing and the curse of seeing what no one else could see—only Cassandra immediately realized who they were and what burden they were carrying home.

An agonizing pain sliced through her body as if she had been struck by lightning, making her cry out so loudly that her voice was heard right across the city.

"Men and women of Troy, come and greet Hector as you greeted him in the past, when he returned from his battles as the victor, bringing joy to your hearts."

The Trojans left whatever they were doing and ran to the gate. One or two of the women were carrying their babies. They wept, they cursed fate, they tore at their hair and tried to get close to the dead man to clasp his head in their hands. Andromache, Hector's wife, led the way along with Hecuba, his mother, and everyone made room for them with tears in their eyes.

They could have stood there at the gate all day, but
Priam wanted to take his son home. The wheels of the cart
began to turn, and the people stepped aside. Priam needed
to be alone with Hector, if only for a little while.

The old king was exhausted. His servant helped him to
lay the bier on a bed, then withdrew. Priam was afraid to lift
the sheet covering his son. What did he look like beneath
the shroud? Would his face and body be familiar, or did he
resemble a lump of meat?

With his heart in his mouth he moved the sheet aside
and stared in astonishment. There lay his son, his firstborn,
beautiful and magnificent, not a scratch to be seen. No
vultures, no dogs had touched him. Even the fatal wound in
his neck had healed.

"You are as beautiful in death as you were in life. You
will be an adornment in the world of the shadows, whither
we are all bound," Priam said. He kissed his son on the lips,
then called the people in.

Andromache with the coal-black hair and the lily-white
arms placed her hand on the body and raised her voice.

"My husband, you have died too young and left me
alone with our son. He is only a little boy, who may not
grow up to be my solace. Our city will be laid waste now
you are no longer here to defend it and us, its people. Men,
women, and children will be hustled onto the Achaeans'
hollow ships, I among them. Our son will be enslaved,

unless some hotheaded Achaean hurls him from the tower in revenge because you, his father, killed so many of them. You showed no mercy in this dreadful war. Now the people mourn your death, and your parents are crushed with grief. But the bitterest sorrow is mine. I have been left alone, I was not there when you died—I did not see you reach out to me from your deathbed, you never said those last words that would carry me through the days and nights for the rest of my life."

Thus she spoke, then made way for Hecuba. It was her turn to bid farewell to Hector. The women all around lamented quietly.

Hecuba was old, but the years had not bowed her back. Instead they carried her, giving her strength and stature.

"My son, you have always occupied the dearest place in my heart, and the gods too have cared for you, not only when you were alive but also in death. Achilles has robbed me of several of my other children and sold them into slavery on the islands of Samos, Imbros, and inaccessible Lemnos. He slew you, as you had slain his friend. He dragged your body along the ground around the funeral mound, but Patroclus did not rise from the dead. You, however, lie here with your cheeks as rosy as if you had died in your sleep."

She was unable to continue, but was overcome by helpless sobbing. The women gently led her away and sat down with her to share her pain.

Helen hesitated. Did she have the right to speak, she who was the cause of all this misery? Andromache understood, and whispered to her, "You have as much right to take your leave of him as everyone else."

Helen stepped forward. She and the dead man were the most attractive individuals in the room.

"Hector, you were the closest to me of all the Trojans, even if it was Paris who brought me here and made me his wife. Would that I had died before this happened! More than ten years have passed since I abandoned my country, and you have never uttered a harsh word to me. You even stopped the others if they started to criticize me. You always had a kind phrase on your lips and a gentle smile in your eyes when we met. Now I weep over you and my wretched fate in despair. No one in this city with its wide streets will forgive me. Only you. No one else."

Thus spoke Helen, and the women in the room lowered their heads and wept with her.

Then it was time for the men to head off into the mountains to gather wood for the pyre. They were worried that the Achaeans might be lying in wait, but Priam assured them that Achilles would not let anything happen to them.

For nine days the Trojans transported newly felled oaks, cedars, and birch trees. On the tenth day, just before dawn, they carried the dead man out and laid him on the pyre.

The old king, whose hands trembled like the flames of the torches, lit the fire with tears in his eyes.

Later that day the people of Troy gathered and doused the embers with wine. Hector's brothers and friends collected his ashes and placed them in a golden urn, which they covered with soft, glowing red cloths. They lowered the urn into the grave and piled large stones on top of it to create a barrow worthy of the dead man, which would be guarded by selected warriors.

Only then did they return to Priam's palace for a feast that no one would ever forget.

Such were the funeral rites of Hector, tamer of horses.

Miss sat down and wiped her eyes.

"That's it. That's the end of the story," she said.

"Oh no!" the whole class shouted out as one.

She shrugged, as if to say that she couldn't help it.

"What happened next? You can't stop there!" Dimitra said.

"It's not my decision, it's Homer's, and that's where he stopped."

"But why?"

"No one knows. Maybe he was in a hurry to start on his next story."

"We want to hear that one too, Miss Marina," I blurted out.

How I had longed to say her name! I felt as if I had plucked my heart from my breast and exposed it for everyone to see.

Fortunately my classmates didn't care about my heart. They were more interested in Homer's tale.

"We want more, we want more!" they chanted.

Miss let us carry on making a fuss for a little while, then she said, with a smile that laid the sky at our feet—well, at mine at least, "That's the first time anyone in the class has said my name. I know you call me the Witch."

We were a little embarrassed. It was true. We did call her the Witch, because the village's bad-tempered, cowering dogs would stop barking as soon as she appeared.

She turned to me.

"Would you please say it again, so I can enjoy it?"

I didn't take much persuading, and nor did the rest of the class. We shouted "Marina, Marina" as if she were a football team. But she refused to give in as far as the story was concerned. I had the feeling that she was in a hurry to be somewhere else.

"Tomorrow is another day," she said as she waved us off.

Dimitra walked along beside me, but without hopping on one leg from time to time as she usually did.

"Are you upset?" I asked.

"No."

"So what's the matter?"

"Nothing."

I thought for a moment.

"Is it because of what happened yesterday?" I ventured.

"Maybe." After a little while she added: "You'll never love me."

I didn't protest. I couldn't. It was true. She was the loveliest girl in the world, but I couldn't love her. Because I loved someone else, who didn't love me.

"It was worse for the Trojans," I said, and we both burst out laughing.

"Yes, what would we do without Homer?" Dimitra replied, and we parted as the best of friends.

Twenty-one

THE NEXT DAY Miss Marina was like a different person. She was wearing an open-necked dress patterned with great big sunflowers. Her thick black hair was held in place by a golden ribbon, and her eyes shone.

It was one of those heartrendingly beautiful mornings, the kind that makes you want to embrace the whole of creation: the mountain above the village, the lush valley, the olive groves, the vines with their acidic scent.

We opened all the windows in the classroom and Miss took center stage once more. We got to hear the end of the story.

———————————

Troy did not fall after Hector's death. New heroes emerged, including Paris the womanizer, whose skill with the bow made him a nightmare for the Achaeans. Then reinforcements arrived from distant allies, including Ethiopia. The

Amazons came all the way from Thrace, led by Penthesilea, their fierce young queen, and were even more of a nightmare. They were consummate warriors who appeared as suddenly as a storm and rode away with the wind after mowing down their heavy-footed opponents.

Penthesilea and Achilles eventually faced each other man to man, so to speak, and he killed her. However, he died at the hands of Paris, who shot an arrow into his heel—the only part of his body that was vulnerable.

The war did not end, and Briseis buried him, in spite of the fact that he had already left her before his death.

Paris was slain by another skilled bowman, whose arrows caused foul-smelling, incurable wounds. Still Troy resisted, and time was not on the side of the Achaeans. They were exhausted, and they longed to go home. They risked everything on a ruse that Odysseus had come up with: the wooden horse.

The Achaeans pretended to sail away, but they left behind a huge wooden horse, with some of their best warriors hiding in its belly. The Trojans couldn't resist pulling the horse into the city, whereupon they ate and drank to celebrate their victory. When they eventually lay down in their beds, the Achaeans emerged from inside the horse and slaughtered them as they slept.

Menelaus, Helen's betrayed husband, stormed into her chamber with his sword at the ready, determined to kill her and restore his honor by spilling her warm blood on the cold stone floor. She was waiting for him with her hair swept up in "the executioner's style," leaving her neck exposed, and she was wearing a long white dress. She opened it and pointed to her heart.

"This is where the fault lies," she said.

Menelaus the slayer of men was dazzled by her face, her throat, and her bosom, and the sword fell from his hand. Beauty conquered both the man and his rage.

It took the Achaeans several days to destroy the city completely. They razed it to the ground, and only Hecuba could be seen wandering the deserted streets singing her mournful songs.

How did it go for those who had survived that terrible war?

Andromache was forced to go with Achilles's son.

Odysseus began his long journey back to the island of Ithaca.

Agamemnon was murdered by his wife when he arrived home.

Homer didn't care about any of this. He wanted to talk about one thing and one thing only: the fact that war is a source of tears, and that there can be no victors.

———————

The siege of Troy was over.

The war in which we were living went on.

We were on our way home when British planes appeared over the village. The German airfield was set on fire. A plane that managed to take off was immediately shot down. It landed in the middle of the square, where people had gathered as usual. Many died, and several more were injured.

Dimitra's father—who became twice himself when he was drunk—was struck in the middle of the forehead by a piece of metal and died instantly. Dimitra suffered a deep laceration in her right thigh.

Miss Marina was shot as she ran to the wreckage of the plane to help Wolfgang out. They died in the flames together.

That was the last day of the great war.

It was also the last war for my father. My grandmother eventually found out that he had died in jail. No one knew where he was buried or if he had been buried at all.

Maybe he was just tossed into some ravine to feed the vultures and the wolves.

We never got to say goodbye to him.

I never got to hear his last words.

Instead I had to take care of my mother.

But I wasn't alone. In the end Dimitra and I became what we were meant to be. We became a couple. I went to her house every day and helped her take a few steps.

"You're my crutch," she would say.

I knew I was more than that.

I also knew she was my crutch.

It wasn't long before a new war began.

The worst war of all. Greek against Greek, brother against brother, father against son.

The Trojan War had simply changed its name.

Dimitra and I would survive this too.

Every Sunday afternoon we went to the churchyard and tended the graves. Dimitra's father was lying there, Miss Marina was lying there.

In the distance we could see the village, with the lamps being lit one by one.

Our mothers were waiting for us.

AFTERWORD

Ever since I was in high school *The Iliad* has touched my imagination and aroused my admiration. In my eyes it is the strongest anti-war poem ever written. Unfortunately a great many people find it difficult to read. There is nothing wrong with the translations. The problem is that these days we do not stimulate, do not enable the demanding reading that *The Iliad* offers.

For several years I wondered whether it might be possible to do something about that—which is what I have tried to do now. Blasphemy? Perhaps. Hubris? No. I had absolutely no intention of trying to replace Homer.

I just wanted more people to get to know him.

The reader must decide whether I have succeeded.

Two individuals have contributed well-founded and insightful comments: my friend and colleague Ernst Brunner, and Ida Östenberg, Associate Professor of Classical Archaeology and Ancient History.

Warm and heartfelt thanks to you both.

Theodor Kallifatides
Bungenäs, Sweden, August 21, 2017